Kristy and Mr. Mom

Kristy and Mr. Mom
Ann M. Martin

AN
APPLE
PAPERBACK

SCHOLASTIC INC.
New York Toronto London Auckland Sydney

Cover art by Hodges Soileau

ISBN 0-590-48225-4

12 11 10 9 8 7 6 5 4 3 2 1   5 6 7 8 9 0/0 9

Printed in the U.S.A.   40

First Scholastic printing, January 1995

The author gratefully acknowledges
Jahnna Beecham
and
Malcolm Hillgartner
for their help in
preparing this manuscript.

Kristy and Mr. Mom

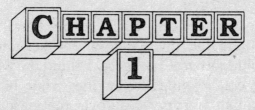

CHAPTER 1

RRREEOWW!

I sat bolt upright in my bed. This was not an ordinary Saturday morning. Something very strange was happening outside. It sounded as if a cat had gotten its tail caught in some door.

I stumbled to my bedroom window and peered outside. The world had been painted white.

"Snow!" I gasped. "When did that happen?"

Snow's not unusual for winter in Stoneybrook, Connecticut, but the day before had been warm and sunny. A blizzard must have hit us while I was asleep.

RRREEOW!

The high-pitched whine was coming from the spinning wheels of my stepfather's car. It was stuck fast in a two-foot drift that lined our driveway. Watson Brewer, dressed in a wool topcoat and hat, was trying to push the car out of the drift. I could tell he was putting a lot of effort into it because his face was bright red.

Who was driving? I rubbed my hand in a circle to defog my window. My seventeen-year-old brother, Charlie, sat behind the wheel of the car, revving the engine, while bits of dirt and snow sprayed all over the place.

I chuckled to myself. "Even when you live in a mansion, your car can get stuck."

You see, I haven't always lived in a mansion. I used to live in a little house on Bradford Court with my mom and three brothers: Charlie (the one at the wheel), Sam, age fifteen, and David Michael, age seven and a half. Who am I? Kristy Thomas. I'm thirteen and in the eighth grade at Stoneybrook Middle School. When I was little, my dad walked out on my family, leaving Mom to work and raise four kids by herself. It was a struggle, but Mom's pretty tough, and my brothers and I tried to help out as much as we could.

I loved living on Bradford Court because my best friend, Mary Ann Spier, was my next-door neighbor. And Claudia Kishi, another terrific friend, lived right across the street. If we hadn't all been neighbors, the Baby-sitters

Club probably wouldn't even exist. What's the Baby-sitters Club? Just one of the most important things in my life, that's all. But I'll tell you all about the BSC later.

Where was I? Oh, yeah. While we were living on Bradford Court, Mom met Watson Brewer, a genuine millionaire. I'm not kidding. He is the CEO (Chief Executive Officer) of Unity Insurance, which has its main offices in Stamford. Anyway, after Mom and Watson dated for a while, they fell in love. Before we knew it they were married, and Mom and us four kids joined Watson and his two kids who live with him every other month, four-year-old Andrew and seven-year-old Karen, in the mansion on McLelland Street.

Karen and Andrew are terrific. Karen is bright (she has already skipped a grade in school), reads like crazy, and has a tremendous imagination. She makes up great ghost stories and almost convinced me that our next-door neighbor, Mrs. Porter, is a witch named Morbidda Destiny.

While Karen is outgoing, Andrew can be pretty shy. And though he's not athletic as I am, he tries hard. During our Mini-Olympics he entered every event and won the "Most Determined" award.

After Mom and Watson got married, they

adopted two-year-old Emily Michelle from Vietnam. Soon after that, my grandmother, Nannie, moved in too, to help out. So when Andrew and Karen are here ten people live in our house. Ten people, plus the Brewer/Thomas zoo. Boo-Boo, Watson's extremely large cat, who is practically as big as a person. And Shannon the Bernese mountain dog puppy, who thinks she's a person. Finally, our two goldfish, Crystal Light the Second and Goldfishie, and two pets that travel back and forth with Karen and Andrew, a rat named Emily Junior, and a hermit crab named Bob.

With that many people and animals, our house can get as hectic as Grand Central Station. Today, however, was just your average mildly crazy day. I threw on a turtleneck, a sweater, and jeans (my friends in the BSC call it my uniform) and hurried downstairs to see what I could do to help out.

Emily Michelle was parked in front of the television in the den, watching cartoons and munching dry Cocoa Puffs out of a bowl. Since she's only two and a half, most of them were spilling onto the carpet. I made a mental note to be sure to clean them up later.

Nannie was in the dining room, listening to one of her favorite CDs while she dusted. It was Frank Sinatra, working up to the big finale

4

to "New York, New York." I caught Nannie waving her dust rag in the air, doing high kicks in time to the music.

Can you tell she's not your average grand-mother-type? She's a bowler *extraordinaire*, a green-thumbed gardener, one fantastic chef, and the owner of possibly the most outrageous car in Stoneybrook — the Pink Clinker. I'm nuts about her. And so's everyone else. Her list of friends is very long and includes the grocers, folks from her old neighborhood, and practically everyone she's helped as a volunteer at the hospital.

My brother Sam was in the mudroom, putting on his coat and gloves, getting ready to head off to his part-time job at the grocery store.

"Cock-a-doodle-doo! I'm a musician, too!" David Michael suddenly leapt in front of me. He had his hands tucked under his armpits and was flapping his elbows like wings.

"David Michael!" I said, putting my hand on my chest. "You scared me."

"I'm not supposed to be scary on those lines," he said, dropping his arms to his sides. "I'm supposed to sound friendly. The director said so."

David Michael has been bitten by the acting bug. And he's got it bad. Ever since he played

5

a Winkie in his school production of *The Wizard of Oz*, all he ever talks about is the theatre. When our community theatre announced they were doing *The Brementown Musicians* as their winter children's show, he begged to be allowed to audition. He was cast as the rooster, and all we've heard for the past week is, "Cock-a-doodle-doo! I'm a musician, too!" It's enough to drive anyone batty.

"Look, David Michael, if the director wants you to be more friendly, why don't you try smiling when you say your line?" I suggested. "You could even do a friendly little rooster bow at the end of it."

David Michael's face lit up. "Thanks, Kristy. I knew you'd be able to help me."

He raced into the dining room, where we have a huge gilt-edged mirror hanging over the sideboard, and practiced smiling and bowing. Nannie swept by between kicks and gave him a few swipes with the dust rag. Didn't I tell you it was a madhouse here? And it's like this practically every day.

"Kristy!" Mom called from the top of our huge staircase. "Watson is out there in the snow with no boots or gloves on, trying to get his car unstuck. Why don't you and Sam see if he could use some more help?"

Sam heard his name mentioned and stepped

into the entry hall. "I tried to help but Watson said he didn't need any."

"Well, he does." Mom put her hands on her hips. "You tell him if he doesn't let you push that car, I'm coming out to do it."

Sam grinned and saluted. "Yes, ma'am." Then he marched like a soldier toward the front door.

"Wait for me!" I grabbed my parka from the closet and ran out behind him. I'm extremely athletic (being coach of the Kristy's Krushers softball team, I'd better be) and I figured I could probably be as useful as Sam.

"All right, Charlie," Watson called. "Try her again. Only this time don't gun it."

Big clouds of exhaust billowed out from behind the car as the tires spun uselessly in the snow.

"Hey, Watson!" Sam tapped him on the shoulder. "Why don't you take a rest, and Kristy and I will push."

Watson leaned over with his hands on his knees and tried to catch his breath. "Thanks, Sam. I have to admit I'm feeling a little winded."

It really surprised me to hear him say that. Watson doesn't like to admit defeat — which is probably why he's been so successful with his insurance company.

Sam tapped on the driver's window and Charlie rolled it down. "Charlie, put it in neutral, and Kristy and I will push it out of the drift to a place that's less slick. This patch is solid ice."

"Gotcha!"

I spread some gravel (from one of the planters by the front entrance) on the ground behind the bumper of the car to give Sam and me some traction. Then we braced ourselves against the trunk of the car.

"On the count of three," Sam said, huffing, as we rocked the car back and forth.

"One, two — "

We didn't even reach three. The car bumped up over the snow drift and coasted the rest of the way down the icy drive. At the bottom, Charlie put on the emergency brake and hopped out, holding the door for Watson.

Watson was still standing back where the car had been stuck. He took a crisp white handkerchief out of his suit pocket and dabbed at his forehead. Little beads of sweat had formed on his brow and I noticed that his face was still flushed. I made a mental note to tell Mom to urge him to take it easy.

Then he picked up his briefcase and smiled at the three of us. "Thanks, kids. I guess I've gotten a little out of shape. Too much time at the computer terminal and not enough time in the fresh air."

"No kidding." Charlie punched him playfully on the shoulder. "Why are you going to work on Saturday, anyway?"

"We're opening a new branch office in Houston and I need to go over the architectural plans." Watson smiled as he settled into the driver's seat and buckled up. "Don't worry, I haven't become a workaholic. I'll be home in time for the football game this afternoon. And remember, Charlie, it's your turn to make the popcorn."

As I watched Watson drive away, I got a very odd feeling inside. I figured it was because I hadn't eaten breakfast, so I shrugged it off.

"Well, I have to get to the store," Sam said, hurrying off down the street. "Dave's going to drive me there. See you guys later."

Charlie and I waved good-bye, and as we walked back toward the house I reminded him of my baby-sitting job that afternoon. "You're supposed to drive me to Karen and Andrew's, remember?"

"It's right up here." He tapped his forehead. "Besides, I promised them I'd give them a ride in the Junk Bucket."

The Junk Bucket is Charlie's name for his old beat-up car. It's a classic!

When the two of us stepped back inside the house, David Michael was posed on the stairs, crowing like a rooster at the top of his lungs. Nannie was cleaning the rug in the hall, using the vacuum cleaner as a dance partner. In the den, Emily Michelle carefully crunched the spilled cocoa puffs with her toes.

Charlie looked at me and shook his head. "This isn't a house, it's a lunatic asylum."

"Yeah." I grinned back at him. "Situation, normal."

CHAPTER 2

"You're not serious!" Claudia gasped. "Sabrina Bouvier went to the movies with Pete Black? I thought she was going with Carlos Mendez."

"They broke up on Friday," Stacey explained. "Carlos said he wanted to start seeing Susan Taylor."

"Susan Taylor!" Everyone else gasped.

"But she's Sabrina's best friend," Mary Anne sputtered.

Monday meetings of the Baby-sitters Club always start out a little rowdy because we have a whole weekend's worth of news and gossip that we need to catch up on. Gossip can sometimes be fun to hear but, as club president, it's my responsibility to make sure our meetings start and end on time.

"Excuse me? Excuse me?" I raised my voice and shouted, "Listen up, everybody!" I pointed at the clock on Claudia Kishi's bedside table, which had just turned from 5:29 to 5:30. "This meeting of the Baby-sitters Club will now come to order."

Instantly the room fell silent. Stacey did let out one tiny giggle, I guess because I had been a little loud with my announcement (not unusual for this big mouth), but everybody else sat quietly waiting for the meeting to get underway.

Before I go any further, I should tell you what the Baby-sitters Club is and how it began.

I'm proud to say that the club was my idea. It hit me like a bolt of lightning one day, when we were still living in the old house on Bradford Court. I was listening to my mom make call after call to find a sitter for David Michael. She was really losing patience, and I didn't blame her. I thought, *Wouldn't it be great if she could call one number and reach a lot of sitters?* That's when it hit me.

The Baby-sitters Club!

The first thing I did was call my best friend Mary Anne Spier, and tell her about it. She thought it was a great idea. Next we told Claudia Kishi, who thought it wasn't just a great idea, it was awesome. Then Claudia suggested we invite this new girl, Stacey McGill, to join us. And that's how the BSC began.

At first it was just the four of us. I was elected president because the club had been my idea, and because I have a lot of good leadership qualities. I know how to motivate people to work together and get things done. Okay, I'll admit it, sometimes I go overboard and become totally bossy, but generally my friends call me on it right away.

We decided to hold our meetings in Claudia's room because (are you ready for this?) she not only has her own telephone, but her own personal phone line. (I guess Mr. and Mrs. Kishi were tired of having their phone tied up all the time.) That's the main reason Claud was elected vice-president. Claudia is also the club's artist. She designed our fliers, which we put up everywhere. (Now the club is so successful that we hardly ever need to advertise.)

Claud can usually be found up to her elbows in some new art project, like making papier-mâché earrings, or tie dying T-shirts, or making totally cool collages out of bright paint, foil, and wild pictures clipped from magazine ads. This winter Claud's been into hats. She buys old hats in thrift stores and covers them in sequins, buttons, and really outrageous feathers. Usually she wears them with one of her super-trendy outfits, like a red long underwear shirt with tiny black-and-white polka dot suspenders, pinstripe trousers, and ruby-sequined slippers.

Art is Claud's life. Schoolwork is *not*. Don't get me wrong. Claud's smart. But she really isn't interested in subjects like math and English. And let's face it, she's a pretty awful speller. To make matters worse, her sister, Janine, is a certified genius. I'm serious. She's not only at the top of her class in high school, but she takes college courses at the same time.

Our club treasurer is Claudia's best friend, Stacey McGill. She's a whiz at math, which is a relief to the rest of us. Stacey collects our dues, keeps track of our earnings in the club record book, and pays our bills. (We help pay for Claud's phone line, and now that I've moved, we also pay Charlie, to drive me across town to the meetings.) If we need money to stock our Kid-Kits, Stacey hands it out.

Kid-Kits, by the way, are another one of my great ideas. (Do I sound conceited? I don't mean to.) Kid-Kits are boxes that we decorate any way we like, and then fill with old toys, books, and supplies for activities. Sometimes, as a special treat, we'll take them with us on our sitting jobs. The kids love them.

I told you that Stacey was a math whiz, but did I mention that she's gorgeous? Blonde, curly hair, piercing blue eyes, and a built-in sense of style that is totally sophisticated. And why not? She grew up in a New York City neighborhood, where there is a super-trendy boutique on every corner. That's probably where she developed her favorite hobby — shopping 'til she drops!

Because she's so cool and gorgeous and friendly Stacey has never lacked for boy-friends. She even dated my brother Sam for awhile. But I'd have to say that her dating days are over, at least for now. Ever since she met Robert, it's been Luv with a capital L. Frankly I don't go in for all that goopy stuff. I hang out with Bart Taylor, captain of the Krushers' rival softball team, Bart's Bashers. We like each other a lot but we don't go around all dewy-eyed like Stacey and Robert.

It sounds as if Stacey has the perfect life, doesn't it? Far from it. First of all Stacey has this very serious disease, diabetes. That means her body can't control the level of sugar in her blood. It also means that she always, *always* has to watch her diet. Sweets are a giant no-no. She also has to give herself insulin injec-tions every day. I would call myself a pretty brave person, but I don't know if I'd have the courage to stick myself with a needle every morning. (Ew!)

As if her medical problems weren't enough to handle, Stacey's parents are divorced. But Stacey hasn't let any of that get to her. She's always bright and cheery, and a real plus to our club.

Just as the office of treasurer needs someone with good math sense, the office of secretary needs a person with great organizational skills and good handwriting. My best friend, Mary Anne Spier, fits that description to a tee. She schedules every one of our sitting jobs, re-members all of our outside conflicts (such as orthodontist appointments, ballet lessons, or softball practice), and keeps track of things in our record book. Guess how many mistakes she's made? Zero. And I bet she never will.

People are usually surprised that we're best friends because in many ways we are total, complete opposites. While I'm outgoing and love groups of people, Mary Anne is shy and wilts at big parties. My hobbies are sports, sports, and more sports. Mary Anne loves to knit and read. She's a very caring person. Sometimes too caring. When we were little and I climbed a tree, Mary Anne would stand at the bottom, wringing her hands with worry that I was going to fall out of it. She's also about the most emotional person on the planet. I've watched her cry over the kittens in cat food commercials. And speaking of kittens, one of the lights of Mary Anne's life is her gray striped kitten, Tigger.

Sometimes I think Mary Anne's so sensitive because she spent a lot of time by herself when she was younger. You see, Mary Anne's mom died when Mary Anne was really little, so her father had to raise her by himself. I think he was a little too strict. Her dad used to insist that Mary Anne come straight home from school, and he only let her talk on the phone if it was about homework. Plus, he made her dress in really babyish clothes and wear her hair in pigtails until she was nearly thirteen.

But all of that has changed. In fact, I'd have to say that in the last year or so, Mary Anne's life has been turned upside down.

I think it all started with a baby-sitting experience. Mary Anne was sitting for Jenny Prezzioso, who came down with a fever of a hundred and four. It was really scary for Mary Anne because she couldn't reach the Prezziosos or her own dad. Finally she called 911, and the ambulance came and took Jenny to the hospital. Luckily, Jenny turned out to be okay. Mary Anne's dad was really proud of her for

17

handling the situation in such a grown-up way. After that, he loosened up. Now Mary Anne chooses her own clothes and wears her hair the way she wants.

Logan Bruno has had a big effect on Mary Anne's life, too. It's funny that Mary Anne, who is definitely the shyest member of our club, was the first to have a steady boyfriend. But Logan is a great guy. And really perfect for Mary Anne, too. He's cute (Mary Anne thinks he looks like her favorite TV star, Cam Geary), friendly, and manages to charm everyone with his Kentucky accent. He's an associate member of the BSC (which means he doesn't attend regular meetings, but is on call if we need him). Logan and Mary Anne have had their ups and downs but all in all, I'd say they are pretty devoted to each other.

That brings me to Dawn Schafer, Mary Anne's other best friend. Dawn had just moved here from California with her mom, Sharon, and ten-year-old brother, Jeff, when she met Mary Anne. They instantly became best friends (which was a little hard for me at first, but eventually I realized that a person could have two best friends). Anyway, one night Mary Anne and Dawn were looking through Mrs. Schafer's high school yearbook when they recognized Mary Anne's dad in one of the pictures. They discovered that he and Mrs. Schafer had been a major couple in high school. Isn't that cool?

That's when Dawn and Mary Anne had *their* great idea. They thought, wouldn't it be fun if our parents got together again? So they talked them into meeting for a date. After that it was like a snowball rolling down a hill, growing bigger and bigger. First they dated, then they fell in love all over again. Before Dawn and Mary Anne knew it, they were seated side by side in the front pew at Richard and Sharon's wedding and then — poof! They were stepsisters.

Mary Anne and her dad moved into the Schafers' old farmhouse with Dawn and her mom. (Dawn's brother Jeff had already gone back to California to live with his dad. He'd had a hard time adjusting to school and Connecticut.) Things were a little bumpy at first, because the two households were so different. For one thing, Dawn and her mom are real health-food nuts. Their idea of a treat is a bowl of granola with plain yogurt and a banana. (I prefer something more along the lines of a stack of Oreos and a glass of milk, and so does Mary Anne.) So for a while it was the veg-heads vs. the meat-eaters. But that wasn't the only problem. When it comes to housekeeping, Dawn's mom is pretty casual (some people might even call her a bit of an absent-minded slob). She'll put the wrench in the refrigerator and the milk in the tool box. Mary Anne's dad is Richard the Organized Neatnik. He believes that everything should be labeled and in its proper place. I'm not kidding. He even files his socks. Then there was the Tigger problem. Dawn's mom, Sharon, wasn't exactly crazy about cats. But she finally got used to Tigger, Mr. Spier finally adjusted to their easy-going housekeeping, and all of them sorted out the food situation by compromising.

So at this point, you'd expect me to say they all lived happily ever after, right? Wrong. After a while Dawn began to miss her dad, her brother, and her friends in California. She finally became so homesick that she decided to go back there to live.

Talk about a major shock! All of us in the BSC missed her terribly. We felt as if a giant hole had appeared in our lives. We wrote lots of letters and made a ton of calls, but it still wasn't the same as having her with us.

Out in California, Dawn freaked a little when she discovered that her dad was serious about his girlfriend, Carol. It upset her so much that she hopped a plane without telling anyone, and came back to Connecticut. That made both of her parents furious. They were so mad that they sent Dawn back to California without letting her visit any of us. (They couldn't stop her from seeing Mary Anne, but that's because they live in the same house.)

Anyway, during the next several months, Dawn got more and more involved with her California baby-sitting club, the We ♥ Kids Club, and she was even a bridesmaid at her dad's wedding. (Yup, he married Carol.)

Boy was that a crazy month. You see, Mrs. Barrett, one of our favorite clients here in Stoneybrook, needed the BSC's help with her own wedding. Unfortunately, she decided to get married on the very same day as Dawn's father. Suddenly we had two weddings on opposite coasts to worry about. We finally worked it out. Claudia, Mary Anne, and I flew out to California to be with Dawn. And Stacey, Jessi, and Mal stayed in Stoneybrook to help with Mrs. Barrett's wedding.

That brings me to some extremely good news: Dawn finally came home. Which was a major cause for celebration! Our alternate officer, Shannon Kilbourne (who's usually an associate member, like Logan), had been great filling in for Dawn, but when Dawn came home Shannon was eager to give her back her old office. You see, Shannon, who lives across the street, is very active in the French Club, at her private school. She is also involved in a lot of extracurricular activities and said she'd like to concentrate on those for a while. But she assured us that she still wants to come to some BSC meetings.

That covers everyone but Jessica Ramsey and Mallory Pike, our junior officers. They're best friends, and because they're so close, I sometimes find myself saying their names as if they were one person: "Mal-and-Jessi." They're in the sixth grade. They love horses and horse books, especially ones written by Marguerite Henry. And they're the oldest kids in their families. That's where the similarities stop.

Here's what makes them different: Mal has red hair, glasses (she's begged for contacts but so far her parents say no way), and braces (they're the clear kind that don't show up too much). Jessi has cocoa-brown skin, black hair (which is usually pulled into a bun, because she's always going to or coming from ballet class), and long dancer's legs.

Mal dreams of being a children's book author and illustrator. She's off to a good start having won "Best Overall Fiction" on Young Author's Day. Jessi dreams of being a prima ballerina in a ballet company in New York. I have no doubt that she'll make it, too. She's already danced the lead in *Coppélia* and *Sleeping Beauty* at her dance school here in Connecticut.

Jessi has a younger sister, Becca, and a baby brother, Squirt. (No, Squirt's not his official name. It's John Philip Ramsey, Jr., which is a big name for such a little guy!) Mal has *eight* kids in her family. Here are their names, from the ten-year-old triplets to the youngest, who's five (I always have to take a deep breath to say them all): Adam, Byron, Jordan — they're the triplets — Vanessa, Nicky, Margo, and Claire. Phew! With Mr. and Mrs. Pike, that brings the total at their dinner table each night to ten, which is a lot of spilled milks and "please, pass the potatoes." (Believe me, I *know*.)

So that's our club. Quite a crew, huh? We meet every Monday, Wednesday, and Friday afternoon from five-thirty until six, to take care of club business, which involves dues paying (boo!) and writing in the club notebook. That was also my idea. Writing a brief description of our baby-sitting jobs is a good way to keep track of what's happening with our clients. We all know if somebody is teething, or having trouble dealing with a new baby sister, or worrying about the Toilet Monster. (I'm not making that one up. It's in the notebook.)

Brring!

Five-thirty-two and already the phone was ringing. I had a feeling it was going to be a busy meeting.

"I'll get it." Jessi gracefully dove for the phone. "Baby-sitters Club. This is Jessi."

We listened as Jessi took the information from the caller. "Tuesday afternoon, from three-thirty to five-thirty. All right. We'll call you right back." Jessi hung up. "That was Mrs. Marshall. She needs a sitter for tomorrow."

Mary Anne checked the schedule book. "Stacey has her doctor's appointment, Claud has Art Club and I'm taking care of the Hills. So that leaves Kristy and Dawn."

Dawn's face brightened. "Gosh, I haven't even seen the Marshalls in at least six months. I've really missed Nina and Eleanor."

I grinned at Mary Anne and nodded. Mary Anne carefully printed Dawn's name in the ledger. "Then Dawn will take the job with the Marshalls."

Dawn smiled at me and whispered, "Thanks."

I patted her on the shoulder. "It's great to have you home."

Jessi called Mrs. Marshall back to tell her that Dawn would be there tomorrow, and the second she hung up the phone, it rang again. We spent the rest of the half hour taking client calls, making sitting assignments, and paying dues.

Before I knew it, the meeting was over and I still didn't know whether Susan Taylor was really interested in Carlos, or if anything happened with Sabrina and Pete at the movies. I guess that would wait until next time!

CHAPTER 3

"Beep! Beep!"

Charlie hit the horn of the Junk Bucket.

"See you, Charlie!" I shouted, even though I knew he couldn't hear me through the rolled-up car windows. "Thanks."

Charlie had picked me up at Claud's after our BSC meeting and driven me home. He had an intramural game at school, so instead of pulling into the driveway, he just dropped me by the curb.

The roads had recently been plowed and huge mounds of snow lined McLelland Street. It sparkled in the glow of the streetlights. I stared at the wall of white piled between me and the sidewalk. A little more snow had fallen that morning and it was deep. And powdery. I couldn't resist it.

"A-one, a-two, and a-three!" I hurled my

whole body over the snow bank and was instantly buried up to my armpits in snow. "All right!"

I know a lot of people don't like winter, but I love it. I lay back in the snow and waved my arms up and down to make angel wings. I did the same with my legs, making the angel's dress. Then I stood up carefully and leaped as far away from my snow angel as I could. (You have to do that or you'll leave big footprints in the angel's dress.)

"Careful, Kristy, the sidewalk is extremely icy."

"Watson?" I peered down the drive. "What are you doing out here?"

"I thought I'd finish clearing the drive tonight," he said, scraping a snow shovel along the concrete drive. "That way I won't have to worry about it tomorrow morning."

"Shouldn't Charlie or Sam be doing that?" I asked.

Watson rested one elbow on top of the shovel handle. "They had school activities, so I told them not to worry about it."

He was out of breath and his face was almost as flushed as it had been that morning. I have to admit, it worried me to see him so red-faced. I put my hand on the shovel. "There's a football game on tonight. If you toss a frozen pizza in the oven, I'll finish the rest of the driveway."

Watson handed over the shovel. "It's a deal."

He took a handkerchief out of his parka pocket and dabbed at his shiny forehead. "This shoveling really has me winded. I feel like I've just cleared the entire town of Stoneybrook." He shook his head in dismay. "I'm going to have to spend a little more time at the gym. Get my stamina up."

I watched him mop his forehead a few more times. Sweat was just pouring off him. "Gee, Watson, you don't look so good," I said. "I wonder if you're coming down with the flu or something."

He took a deep breath. "Maybe I am. I feel like I have a fever and my stomach is kind of upset. Maybe I'll go inside and sit for a minute."

I watched Watson trudge through the snow to the door of our house. The way he was walking, all hunched over, made him look like an old man. Which he is not. He paused at the top of the porch steps to catch his breath again, then turned and waved. "I'll have the pizza waiting for you."

"Thanks, Watson." As I bent over the

shovel, I heard a clunk. When I looked up again, Watson had fallen to his knees on the porch and was clutching his chest.

"Watson!" I screamed.

My voice echoed in my ears as I dropped the shovel and ran for the porch. Everything seemed to move in slow motion. Watson's eyes were squeezed shut and his face was twisted with pain. I stumbled up the steps, falling at his feet. "Watson, what's the matter?" I cried.

"My chest," he gasped. "Sharp pain . . . get help."

I half crawled, half ran to the front door. "Mom! Help! Somebody!" I yelled as I raced to the phone. My hands were trembling so much I could hardly make my fingers dial 911. "Mom, *help*!" I screamed up the stairwell.

When the emergency operator answered, I tried to keep my voice from shaking as much as my hands. Tears stung my eyes as I choked out the words, "My father. I think he's having a heart attack. Three-fifty-four McLelland. Hurry, please!"

"We'll send the Quick Response Unit out immediately," the operator said, in a quiet voice. "Now try to stay calm and tell me your name."

I swallowed hard and spoke fast. "My name

is Kristy Thomas. My stepfather Watson Brewer is on the front porch. He's clutching his chest. What do I do?"

"Can you give me your phone number, Kristy?"

I told her, then cried, "Please, help."

"Kristy, is your stepfather breathing?"

"Yes."

"Is he conscious?"

"Yes, but he's in a lot of pain."

"Are you alone?"

"I think my Mom and Grandmother are here. Mom!" I screamed up the stairs again. "Nannie!"

"I want you to make sure your father is lying flat," the operator said. "Get a blanket and cover him up. He needs to be kept warm and still. Can you do that, Kristy?"

"Yes, I think so."

"Good. Go do it now. Don't hang up, just put the phone down. I'll stay on the line until help arrives." Mom came running down the stairs. "Kristy, what's the matter?"

"Watson's on the porch," I answered in a choked whisper. "I think he's having a heart attack. I've called for help."

The color drained from Mom's face but she didn't scream or cry. She just started giving orders. "Pillows. Blankets. Now!"

Nannie, who had been feeding the kids in the kitchen, stuck her head into the hall. "What's all the shouting for?"

"It's Watson!" I pointed to the porch where Mom was helping Watson stretch out. She cradled his head in her lap, and whispered, "Hold on, Watson. Just hold on."

I raced to the cedar trunk in the library to grab the blankets, chanting to myself over and over, "Please make them hurry. Please make them hurry."

I never thought the sound of a siren would make me happy, but when I heard the wail of the ambulance as I came down the stairs, I wanted to jump for joy. I raced onto the porch just as the ambulance rounded the corner. The blue lights were flashing and behind the ambulance came a car from the fire department, with its siren wailing, too.

Nannie, who had been keeping David Michael and Emily out of the way, came out to the porch to see if she could help.

My mother looked up at Nannie and cried, "Oh, Mom!"

That was the only moment I saw her show any of the emotion she must have been feeling. After that, she focused all of her attention on Watson, trying to keep him calm and warm.

Nannie touched me on the shoulder. "Kristy, please look after David Michael and Emily," she said quietly. "I'll help your mother."

David Michael and Emily were in the living room, watching the flurry of activity through the big picture windows. Their eyes were wide as saucers and neither one said a word. I knelt between them and hugged them for all I was worth. "He'll be okay," I whispered. "I just know it."

The paramedics worked fast. In minutes, Watson was on a stretcher and being wheeled toward the waiting ambulance. He had an IV in one arm and an oxygen mask over his nose and some sort of heart monitor attached to his chest. Mom held his right hand and ran alongside the stretcher, never once taking her eyes off his face.

As strong as Mom appeared, I realized she must be in shock herself, because she climbed into the ambulance in her house slippers, without a coat.

I ran to the hall closet and grabbed her coat and purse. Nannie appeared and took them from me. "Thanks, Kristy. I'm going to follow the ambulance to the hospital and stay with your mother. Please watch the kids. I want you to call the school and tell Charlie and Sam what's happened. And can you call Karen's and Andrew's mother?"

I swallowed hard. "Yes, I think so."

Nannie squeezed me hard. There were tears in her eyes as she said in a husky voice, "That's my girl."

Then Nannie put on her own coat and knelt down by Emily and David Michael. "You kids help Kristy. Just remember that I love you, and Mommy and Watson love you."

"Is Watson going to be okay?" David Michael asked, his chin quivering.

Nannie nodded firmly. "Of course he is." She gave them each a kiss and ran for the door. "I'll call you the minute I know anything."

That reminded me of the operator on the phone. I thanked her for her help and hung up.

Brrring! The phone rang immediately. It was Shannon from across the street.

"Kristy, I saw the ambulance. What's the matter?"

"It's Watson. He's having a heart attack."

"I'm so sorry. What can I do to help?"

"Shannon, I'm really scared," I said in a rush. "Nannie went with Mom and Watson, and I'm supposed to take care of the kids and call Sam and Charlie."

"I'll call them," Shannon said firmly. "Where are they?"

"At the intramural basketball game at Stoneybrook High School."

"I'll call the school and then I'll be right over to help you with the kids."

"Thanks, Shannon," I said gratefully. "Thanks a lot."

Her call had snapped me back into action. I walked Emily and David Michael to the kitchen and sat them down at the table. "You guys haven't finished your dessert," I said, in the cheeriest voice I could muster.

"I don't feel much like eating," David Michael said quietly.

"I'll bet by the time you finish that piece of pie, we'll get a call from the hospital," I said confidently. "It'll be Mom, and she'll say everything's fine."

He studied my face suspiciously. "You sure?"

"Of course I am." I tried to sound as confident as possible. "And I just came up with a great idea."

"What?" Emily and David Michael were used to my ideas and looked forward to them.

"After you finish your pie, we'll put together a Get Well Quick basket for Watson," I explained. "We can put in some of his fa-

34

vorite things, and some of ours."

"Like my Mighty Men fighting team?" David Michael suggested, his eyes lighting up.

"Sure. Watson will love them."

"Teddy bear!" Emily said gleefully

"I'll put in Mom and Watson's wedding picture," I said, "and that picture we took last summer at the family picnic."

"Boo-Boo?" Emily asked.

I couldn't help chuckling. "No, I don't think they allow cats in a hospital. Especially not big old grumpy ones. How about drawing a picture of Boo-Boo, in a card?" I suggested. "You both can draw one."

That seemed to cheer up the kids. While David Michael chattered about what else to put in the Get Well Quick basket, I called Karen's and Andrew's mom, Lisa, and broke the news.

Basically, I told her what had happened and that I would call the second I heard from Nannie.

"Are you going to be okay over there?" Lisa asked. "Because Seth and I could come over to be with you." Seth is Lisa's second husband. He's a nice man.

"We'll be fine," I assured her. "Sam and Charlie should be home soon, and my friend Shannon is going to come over to help out."

After I hung up the phone I realized that I really could use some more help. Not for baby-sitting but for me. Moral support, I guess. I dialed Mary Anne and Dawn.

"Oh, Kristy," Mary Anne cried when I told her the news. "You must feel just awful."

"I've never felt so scared in my whole life," I admitted. "Or so useless. Mary Anne, there was nothing I could do to help."

"But you did help," Mary Anne protested. "You called the ambulance. You got blankets. Best of all, Nannie knew she could go with your mom and Watson and not have to worry about the younger kids. She trusted that you would be able to look after them. I'd say that's a tremendous amount of help."

"Thanks, Mary Anne. I appreciate that," I murmured. "Look, I better get off the phone. Nannie could be trying to call."

"I'm going to talk to Dad and see if he'll drive us over," Mary Anne said. "At a time like this, you need your friends with you."

The second we hung up, I collapsed on the bench next to David Michael and Emily. I knew I shouldn't cry in front of the kids but hearing Mary Anne say those wonderful things made me want to. I bit my lip hard and told myself, "Everything's going to be okay. It has to be."

36

CHAPTER 4

"I'll get it," David Michael shouted the second the doorbell rang. He raced for the door and I followed, holding Emily by the hand. It was Shannon.

"Kristy!" Shannon gave me a big hug as she stepped inside the house. "I talked to Charlie's and Sam's coach at school. He said he would tell them about Watson at half-time, which should be any minute now."

"Thanks." I led Shannon into the living room where the kids and I had been assembling our supplies for Watson's Get Well Quick basket. My suggestion that we include some pictures had made Emily go wild. She'd grabbed every framed photo from the living room that she could reach, completely clearing the top of the grand piano, plus all of the end tables and bookshelves. It was lucky Shannon arrived when she did or Emily might have started pulling out the photo albums.

"We're putting together a get well basket to take to Watson," I explained.

"Oh?" Shannon cocked her head. "Did the hospital call?"

"No. But we've decided he's going to be okay," I said firmly.

Before we could talk more, the doorbell rang again. This time it was Mary Anne and Dawn.

"We came as quickly as we could," Mary Anne said, as she and Dawn hurried into the foyer. "Dad was a little reluctant to bring us. He thought we might be in the way."

"Mary Anne explained that you were by yourself," Dawn added, "and that you needed our help, so he gave in right away."

"What's the word from the hospital?" Mary Anne asked as she and Dawn followed me into the living room. Shannon was sitting on the floor playing with Emily. David Michael was beside them, trying to choose which deck of cards to include in the Get Well Quick kit — Old Maid or Go Fish.

"I was just telling Shannon that we haven't heard a word, but I'm sure these things take time." I glanced at my watch and saw that it was a little after eight o'clock. "Gosh, I need to start thinking about putting these guys to bed and getting ready for tomorrow."

38

"Let's make a list of what needs to be done," Mary Anne said. She pulled a notepad and a pen from her pocket and sat down on the couch. "You dictate and I'll write it down."

"Baths for the kids, then bedtime stories." I ticked the items off on my fingers. "Lay out David Michael's and Emily's clothes for tomorrow. Clean up the kitchen. Pick up around the house so Mom won't have to worry about it when she gets home."

"How about school lunches?" Shannon asked. "Do we need to make those?"

I ran one hand through my hair. "Oh, yeah. Let's see, there are four of us."

"I'll take that job," Dawn said, standing up. "Making food is one of my favorite hobbies."

"Terrific," Mary Anne joked. "Everyone's going to have sprout sandwiches and carrot juice."

Shannon, Mary Anne, and I looked at each other and wrinkled our noses. "Ew!"

That made everyone giggle. I have to admit I needed to laugh. And it was great having Dawn back. We'd missed her.

"I'll clean the kitchen," Shannon volunteered, "and pick up the downstairs."

"If you take care of the baths," Mary Anne told me, "I'll lay out their clothes and make sure the second floor is picked up."

"But what about the Get Well basket?" David Michael asked with a worried frown. "Who's going to work on that?"

I gave him a hug. "That's your job," I said. "You've chosen the pictures. Before we go to sleep tonight, why don't we pick out a few books, and one of your games? Then tomorrow after school, we can take the basket over to Watson at the hospital."

I saw Mary Anne and the others exchange concerned looks, and I knew exactly what they were thinking. What if Watson didn't make it? Then all of this planning for a Get Well kit would only make things worse. But I wasn't about to let myself think that way. I looked at my friends and said, "It's important that we think positively. All of us."

Time seemed to crawl. I gave Emily her bath and made sure David Michael took his, saw them into their PJs and even put Emily to bed. But still the phone didn't ring.

"Maybe we should call the hospital," I finally said to Mary Anne, who was laying out David Michael's clothes for the next day.

"Didn't Nannie say she'd call the minute she knew anything?" Mary Anne asked.

I nodded. "I just don't know if I can stand to wait much longer." I was about to reach for the phone, when I heard the front door close, and deep voices echo in the foyer.

"Charlie? Sam?" I called from upstairs. "Is that you?"

"Yeah, we're home," Charlie called back.

"How's Watson?" Sam yelled as they ran upstairs. "Is he okay?"

My brothers met me in the hall outside David Michael's room. While Mary Anne read to David Michael, I told them everything that had happened, starting from the moment Charlie dropped me at the curb. I went through every detail of Watson's heart attack, ending with his being rushed to the hospital in the ambulance.

Both of them wanted to go over to the hospital that second, but I managed to convince them to hold off until we'd heard from Nannie. Reluctantly, they went downstairs to the family room to wait.

I ducked my head back into David Michael's room and saw that Mary Anne had things under control. When I checked on Emily, she was fast asleep, so I went downstairs.

"Look," Dawn said when I came into the kitchen. She held up a plate of sandwiches. "I've made three choices. Tuna, ham-and-cheese, and PBJs. With apples and little bags of potato chips." She grinned and said, "I'll have you know there's not a sprout or a drop of carrot juice in sight."

"Thanks, Dawn," I said. "That's a big help. And Shannon did a terrific clean-up job."

Charlie stuck his head in the kitchen. "Did I hear the phone ring?"

"I wish," I replied.

"What time is it now?" Sam asked, joining Charlie in the doorway.

"Sam!" Charlie blew his hair off his forehead in exasperation. "That is the millionth time you've asked me that. It's two minutes later than it was two minutes ago."

This waiting was getting on our nerves. I checked the clock on the microwave. "It's nearly nine-thirty," I said. "Gee, they should know something by now."

"That's it," Charlie yelled, throwing up his arms. "I'm calling the hospital."

Just then the back door opened, and Nannie stepped inside. None of us spoke as she stomped her boots on the rug by the back door, unwound her muffler and took off her wool cap. I don't know about Charlie or Sam, but I was holding my breath, waiting to hear the news.

When Nannie finally looked up and saw our anxious expressions, her face broke into a big smile. "He's fine," she announced. "The heart attack was a mild one."

"All right!" Sam and Charlie gave each other high fives. I hugged Dawn and then we all hugged Nannie.

Shannon and Mary Anne heard the commotion and rushed to join us. "Well?" Mary Anne asked.

"He's okay," I sang out. I could feel my grin pulling at my ears, it was so wide. "Watson's going to be okay."

"However, he is going to have to make some major changes," Nannie added. "He has to exercise, change his diet, and cut out stress."

"When can he come home?" I asked eagerly.

"I'm not sure." Nannie said, running her hands through her hair. She looked wiped out. "Probably not for a while. They have him in intensive care right now, but he should move to a regular room in a few days."

"How's Mom holding up?" Charlie asked.

"She's exhausted," Nannie said. "But relieved that he's going to get better. She decided to stay with him tonight. I told her I'd come back here and make sure everything's okay on the homefront. How did you all do?"

I gave my report, making sure to mention that Dawn had made the lunches, Shannon had cleaned up the kitchen, and Mary Anne had helped with the kids and straightened the rooms upstairs.

"It sounds like you did just fine without me," Nannie said, giving my arm a squeeze. "I'm very proud of all of you."

After I called Karen and Andrew's mom to give her the update, we moved to the living room and talked for another half hour. Nannie gave us all the details of Watson's ordeal. Charlie told Nannie that we had been going nuts not knowing anything.

"I know it was hard for you," Nannie said. "But believe me, we were as much in the dark sitting in that hospital waiting room as you were here at home."

Then Nannie stood up and yawned. "We've all had one rough evening. I think it's time everyone got to bed."

Shannon said, "I have an early morning French Club meeting tomorrow, but I'll check in after school to see if you need me."

"Thanks, Shannon." Nannie smiled warmly. "Give your parents my best."

It was really getting late. Since our house has plenty of bedrooms I suggested Mary Anne and Dawn sleep over. Nannie called their parents to ask permission and then we got ready for bed.

Normally when friends spend the night, I

like to stay up and talk. Not this night. I found some extra nightgowns for Dawn and Mary Anne, showed them their room, and said good night. I fell into bed exhausted and slept like a rock till morning.

I'm glad Mary Anne and Dawn stayed the night, because trying to get David Michael dressed, fed, and off to school in snow gear was a major ordeal for me. Dawn and Mary Anne helped Emily get dressed and fed, while Nannie made calls to the hospital, relatives, and Watson's business.

Sam waited with David Michael at the school bus stop in front of our house. But just as the bus rounded the corner, David Michael remembered that he'd forgotten his script. He made Sam hold the bus while he raced to find it.

"Script?" I repeated, when he came running back into the house. "What script?"

He looked crestfallen. "For play practice after school. *The Brementown Musicians*. I'm the rooster, remember?"

"Oh." I vaguely recalled him showing me his part on Saturday. "Of course. That's very important. I'll bet the script's in the family room."

It took a little bit of searching but we finally found it. In the meantime, Dawn and Mary

Anne needed to go back to their house to get dressed for school. They caught a ride with Charlie.

I took the time after they'd gone to assemble our Get Well Quick Kit for Watson. I used a basket from the Easter supplies stored in the attic. Nannie even added a few goodies, including a book called *Eating Right for the Rest of Your Life*.

"There's no time like the present to change your life," Nannie said. "And he's going to have to start right now. While he's in the hospital."

"In the hospital?" I repeated.

"Of course. Watson has been working too hard lately. I know him. The minute he's able to sit up in bed, he'll be on the phone with his office. It's up to us to make sure he doesn't do that."

"How can we stop him?" I asked, slipping the photos, books, and games into the basket.

"I'm not sure." Nannie put her arm around me and smiled encouragingly. "But for now, we need to send positive thoughts his way so that he can get well as soon as possible."

I had to run to catch my bus. All the way to school, I thought about Watson, and all through homeroom, math, and English, too.

I really did drift through the day like a zombie. I don't remember who I talked to or what happened in any of my classes. At lunch I didn't even notice my food. My attention was focused on the problem of Watson, and how we could help him get better.

Then the last bell rang, and school was finally out. I hurried to the steps in front of SMS and waited impatiently for Charlie to pick me up and drive us to the hospital. I couldn't wait to see Watson!

CHAPTER 5

Tuesday

I was prepared to have a blast with Nina and Eleanor Marshall. It'd been many months since I'd seen them. I wondered if Nina still carried Blankie and if Eleanor's eyes were as big and blue as I'd remembered them. Was I surprised. Not just by the Marshalls but by the three extra kids with them.

When Dawn pressed the Marshalls' bell, the door swung open immediately. A dark-haired girl wearing a baseball cap greeted her with a cheery, "Hiya!"

Dawn blinked several times at the stranger and then put her hand to her mouth. "Oops! I'm sorry, I think I've gone to the wrong house." She stumbled backward down the steps, confused. The house *looked* like the Marshall house. And Dawn was certain that Rosedale was their street. Could she have been in California for so long that she forgot where they lived? She spun in a circle trying to get her bearings. "Maybe they moved and nobody told me," she murmured.

"Come in, Dawn!" a voice called. "The kids can't wait to see you."

Mrs. Marshall was waving from the porch of the house Dawn had just visited.

"I'm sorry," Dawn said, running back up the steps. "I didn't recognize the girl who opened the door."

Mrs. Marshall laughed. "That's Moira Phillips. She and her two brothers have come over to play with Nina and Eleanor."

"Oh." Dawn giggled sheepishly. "I thought I'd gone to the wrong house."

"This is the same old place." Mrs. Marshall

gestured for Dawn to enter. "See?"

Dawn stepped into the entryway. Everything was the way she'd remembered it. To the left was the den, with the living room off to the right. The bedrooms were upstairs, and straight ahead were the kitchen and the laundry room. The laundry room had been the site of what became known as Dawn's Disaster.

You see, four-year-old Nina had this badly frayed blanket, Blankie, that she took everywhere — to the playground, to bed, even to school (which caused her some problems).

One day Mrs. Marshall decided it was time to wash Blankie. She ran it through the washer and stuck it in the dryer at the moment Dawn arrived to baby-sit. After Mrs. Marshall left, the dinger on the dryer went off — and disaster struck.

Dawn opened the dryer door and discovered not one, but *hundreds* of blankies. The old gray blanket had disintegrated. Nina was a wreck at first but Dawn, great baby-sitter that she is, thought fast. She tucked little bits of Blankie into Nina's pockets and up her sleeves. She even put a piece of Blankie in her shoe. "Now he'll always be with you," Dawn had told her. "And no one, not even your classmates, will know."

Pretty clever, huh?

Anyway, Dawn was anxious to see the girls. She didn't have to wait long. "Dawn's here," Nina cried, running down the stairs. She wrapped her arms around Dawn's waist. "I missed you."

Two-year-old Eleanor was right behind her sister. She flung her arms around Dawn and sang out, "I miss you, too!"

Dawn ruffled the girls' hair while she listened to Mrs. Marshall's instructions.

"I've got my jazzercise class tonight, and afterward a few of us are going for coffee," she explained. "Here's the number of the health club. I should only be gone about two hours."

"Do you want me to feed the kids dinner?" Dawn asked.

"Oh, thanks for reminding me," Mrs. Marshall said. "I've put a frozen pizza in the oven. Just turn it on and set the timer for twenty minutes. There's apple juice in the fridge, and the kids can have Popsicles for dessert."

Three heads suddenly appeared at the den door. "Come on, Nina," called the little girl who'd answered the front door. "We're playing doll hospital. Yours is really sick."

Dawn looked at the three kids and back at Mrs. Marshall, who had put on her coat and was heading for the front door. "Um, Mrs.

Marshall? Shouldn't those kids be going home now?"

Mrs. Marshall tapped her forehead. "I am forgetting everything today. You see, this is my first jazz class and I'm really excited about it. I'm taking it with my friend, Kendra Phillips. These are her children — Moira, Bryant, and Tyler."

The kids stepped into the entryway as their names were called.

"And how old are you guys?" Dawn asked.

Moira answered for all of them. "I'm seven, Bryant is six, and Tyler's three." As if to confirm it, Tyler held up three fingers.

"They'll be staying here this evening," Mrs. Marshall said.

"The whole time?" Dawn asked, wide-eyed.

Mrs. Marshall smiled. "Yes, I told Kendra it would be fine to bring her kids over here."

"Five kids." Dawn smiled weakly. "Wow."

"Don't worry," Mrs. Marshall said with a wave of the hand. "There's plenty of food for everyone. The pizza is an extra large pie, and I have two full pitchers of juice."

Dawn told me later that she wasn't concerned about the food. She was worried about her ability to handle that many kids at once. But she didn't say that to Mrs. Marshall. She was too startled.

After Mrs. Marshall left, Dawn turned to the children and took a deep breath. "Well, you guys, it looks like we're on our own. What do you want to do?"

"Let's take our dolls to the den," Nina said, pulling on Dawn's arm.

"I want to build a fort in the room upstairs." Bryant moved to the stairs, with Tyler following.

"TV!" Eleanor folded her hands stubbornly across her chest. "I want TV."

"I'm hungry," Moira said. "Let's eat."

"This is going to be worse than I thought," Dawn muttered as she hurried to stop Bryant, who was already heading up the stairs. "Hold it," she said cheerily. "We either all go upstairs, or all stay downstairs."

"Upstairs," Bryant voted.

"Downstairs," Moira and Nina shouted.

"Upstairs!" Bryant and Tyler shouted back as loudly as they could.

Moira, Nina, and Eleanor lined up, shoulder to shoulder. It was boys against the girls. "Downstairs, downstairs, downstairs!"

The boys took a deep breath, ready to yell back even more loudly. Dawn stepped between both groups and put her hands over her ears. "That's e-*nough*!" she shouted loudest of all.

Her outburst startled them into silence, which gave Dawn just enough time to come up with a new solution. "It's time to play Treasure Hunt," she said. "We'll play it for exactly twenty minutes. By that time, the pizza will be ready and we can eat dinner. After dinner, we can build a fort downstairs in the living room, and watch TV and play dolls in the den."

The kids seemed agreeable and Dawn felt relieved.

"All right!" Dawn clapped her hands together. "Everyone wait in the living room while I turn on the oven and then hide the treasure."

She moved toward the kitchen, making some quick calculations in her head. I'm watching a two-year-old, a three-, four-, six-, and seven-year-old, Dawn thought. That means a wide range of attention spans. Moira might sit still while I hide the treasure, but Nina and Tyler will never make it. She nodded her head firmly and said out loud, "Time for the Kid-Kit."

Dawn turned on the oven, set the timer, and hurried back into the living room. "While I hide the treasure, you guys are going to become pirates."

"Pirates?" Nina wrinkled her nose. "They're yucky."

"Pirates are cool," Bryant said. "I want to be a pirate."

"Me too!" cried Tyler.

"I don't wike piwates," Eleanor declared, imitating her sister just as Tyler had imitated his brother. "Yuck."

Meanwhile Moira seemed to be thinking it over. "Okay," she said finally. "But I get to be the pirate queen."

"No!" Eleanor and Nina wailed. "I want to be queen."

Dawn rubbed her right temple. She could feel a gigantic headache coming on. "Look, you guys," she said, setting her Kid-Kit on the table in the kitchen. "I've got these totally cool makeup crayons. Everyone can be a queen, or a king, or prince, or dragon. If you can color it, you can be it."

The makeup crayons came with a book of designs. Dawn flipped through it while the kids peered over her shoulder, calling out, "I want to be that one. No, I want to be that one."

Dawn hurried to the bathroom, where she knew there was a portable makeup mirror on the vanity shelf. Then she ran into the kitchen and filled several small bowls with a little water for the makeup crayons. She turned around in time to catch Eleanor taking a bite out of one of the crayons.

"No, no, Eleanor," Dawn cried. "Crayons aren't good to eat."

Eleanor seemed to agree with her because she spat out the tip of the crayon onto the linoleum floor. "Yuck."

Yuck seemed to be the word for the day. Dawn scooped up the bits of crayon on the floor and dropped them in the wastebasket under the sink.

"Now you guys paint your faces while I hide the treasure," Dawn said. She took a quick look through her Kid-Kit for something that could be the treasure, and found a packet of glossy foil stickers. "Perfect."

The kids were busily dipping their crayons into the water and smearing them onto their faces. They didn't even notice when Dawn sneaked the stickers out of the box and slipped out of the room. She figured she only had a minute or two before some new catastrophe would hit. She was right.

"Give me that mirror, please," she heard Bryant say.

"No." That was Nina.

"But I said please."

"I don't care, I had it first."

"Please!" he bellowed.

"It's my turn," Tyler called over his brother's voice.

"Let him have it," Moira said.

"It's my house," Nina's voice piped up.

"Gimme!" Eleanor cried.

Dawn blew a strand of hair off her forehead, tucked the stickers into the planter by the bookcase in the den, and trotted back into the kitchen. She found herself in the middle of a genuine tug-of-war.

Nina and Eleanor were holding one side of the mirror, while Moira and her brothers clung to the other. The kids' faces were covered with blue and red and green stripes.

"Time out!" Dawn put her hands in a T formation. "Everybody!"

Moira and her brothers let go of the mirror and Nina and Eleanor fell backward onto the floor with a loud, "Ooomph!"

"Way to go, Schafer," Dawn muttered as she carefully removed the mirror from Eleanor's grasp. "This was a really *great* idea."

"Where's the treasure?" Moira asked. "Did you hide it?"

Dawn nodded. "It's in the den. I'm going to count to ten and then — "

"CHARRRRRGGGGE!" The kids bolted out

of the room before Dawn could even finish her sentence. She had planned to do the hunt in an orderly fashion, but it was too late for that. Dawn followed as quickly as she could, but she wasn't quite quick enough.

Moira and Nina had already tossed all of the couch cushions on the floor. Bryant had knocked at least five books off the bookshelves. Tyler was in the process of turning the toy box upside down and dumping everything onto the floor. Eleanor was the only kid who didn't join the hunt. She spied the couch cushions and dove for them.

"Chaos." Dawn shook her head in amazement. "This room is in total chaos."

As thorough as Nina, Tyler, Moira, and Bryant were in their search (they dismantled everything that could be taken apart), it was Eleanor who found the treasure. Of course, it took an accident for her to do it.

"Careful," Dawn warned, as she watched Eleanor bouncing out of control on the cushions. "You could hurt yourself."

On Dawn's last word Moira stepped onto the cushion, which catapulted Eleanor toward the bookcase. She bounced on her bottom, but her elbow knocked against the side of the planter. "Waah!" she wailed, clutching her arm.

The rest of the kids seemed oblivious to Eleanor's cries, which just served as background noise for their own voices.

"Poor Eleanor," Dawn said, picking her up. "Did you bump against that mean old planter?"

Eleanor rubbed her elbow and nodded shakily.

"Show me where it hit you," Dawn said, kneeling beside the planter.

Eleanor pointed to the edge of the ceramic planter and her eyes, still filled with tears, suddenly lit up.

"Tweasure!" she cried gleefully.

"Not fair!" Moira protested. "You cheated and helped her."

A bell dinged loudly from the kitchen.

"What was that?" called Tyler, who was sitting in the middle of a pile of toys.

"The pizza." Dawn sighed with relief. "It's done."

The children pounded past her into the kitchen where they fought over who would sit where, but Dawn hardly noticed their squalling. Barely an hour had passed (although it felt like a lifetime) and Dawn was already growing numb to it.

Once the seating arrangements had been settled and the pizza served, Dawn found a second to relax. She sat on a stool by the kitchen counter and stared at the kids, who chewed contentedly, their faces covered in smudged bright colors.

Three peaceful minutes went by and then a new disaster occurred. When Tyler reached for another piece of pizza, his arm hit his juice glass, which tipped over into Nina's plate, soaking her slice of pizza.

"Yuck!" Nina said. (Didn't I say that was the word for the day?) "My pizza's ruined."

Eleanor picked up her Tommy-Tippee cup and deliberately sprinkled apple juice all over her pizza. "Mine's yucky, too!" she declared proudly.

Bryant thought that was hilarious and promptly poured his juice over Moira's pizza. She was the only one at the table who was *not* amused.

"I'm telling!" she shrieked.

After the first spill, Dawn had grabbed a few dish towels. For the second she grabbed two more. Now she grabbed the whole drawer full, and a few sponges for good measure.

"*Freeze!*" she barked at the kids. They did just that.

"You are all ice statues," she declared. "You cannot move a single muscle until I have wiped off the table. And even then you won't move a muscle until I say the magic word."

Moira, who was still angry, rolled her eyes.

Dawn pointed her finger at Moira and said, in a deep, commanding voice, "Not a move out of you, young lady, or you will be put in the Pit of Despair — " (Dawn gestured to the tiny laundry room) " — for five million years, or ten minutes—whichever comes first."

Moira didn't know if Dawn was kidding. But just in case, she stared straight ahead.

The kids were still holding their frozen positions when Mrs. Marshall and Mrs. Phillips came in.

"I know we're home early," Mrs. Marshall said. "But our class was canceled because of the snow, so Kendra and I went out for coffee and came home. Hope you don't mind."

Are you kidding? Dawn wanted to shout. I've never been so happy to see someone in my entire life. But of course she didn't. Instead, Dawn said, "I don't mind at all. We've had an action-packed hour."

After Mrs. Marshall had paid Dawn (the same amount she would have paid her to sit for just two children), Dawn turned to the kids, who were still holding their frozen statue positions.

"Abracadabra, kah-loo, kah-lee," she changed. "One wave of my hand, and now you are free."

" 'Bye, Dawn!" Nina and the others shouted. "That was sure fun."

On the way home, Dawn reviewed the afternoon. Mrs. Marshall had not told her that she would be sitting for five kids, which was really unfair. But even though she had been unprepared, things had gone as well as could be expected. There hadn't been any real disasters or accidents, for which she was extremely grateful. However, Dawn couldn't help wondering, What if something really bad had happened? How could just one baby-sitter be expected to handle it?

CHAPTER 6

"Hello?"

I peered around the door into Watson's hospital room. The nurse had told us we could visit him one at a time. We drew straws and I came up last. Charlie, then Sam, had been in to see him just moments before. Now it was my turn.

Watson was lying on his bed, with his eyes closed. Across the room the television attached to the wall droned away softly. A tube taped to the inside of his arm led to a clear plastic bottle dangling from a metal stand beside the bed. Next to the stand was a machine with lots of dials and wires that were connected to his chest. I guessed the machine was there to monitor his heart. In the dim light, Watson looked very tired and frail.

I was shocked by how sick he looked. Somehow I couldn't bring myself to walk in. This fragile man in the bed just couldn't be Watson. Watson was always so confident and strong and full of life.

I didn't realize it but I was actually inching back into the hall. I bumped directly into a metal cart filled with dinner trays and it scooted across the hall and crashed into the wall. The loud noise roused Watson and he called out, "Kristy, is that you?"

I plastered a big smile on my face and entered the room. "Yeah, I just stopped by to see if you were up for a game of touch football. A couple of the patients on this floor are putting a team together."

Watson chuckled, which was a relief because when he did, he stopped looking so pale and drawn. "I may have to sit this one out, coach," he cracked. "The doc's given me strict orders to stay on the bench."

"Then I guess you're just going to have to occupy your time with our special Get Well Quick basket." I set it on the edge of his bed. "Charlie, Sam, David Michael, Emily and I put this together for you. We would've delivered it together but the hospital's strict about visitors."

"Let me take a look at that." Watson pushed a little control button that lay next to his pillow and the bed hummed to life. The back raised up and moved him into a sitting position. "What a wonderful gift."

I giggled. "I'm sure you can guess which one of us put the stuffed teddy bear in there. And who thought the Mighty Men fighter patrol would be fun for you."

Watson handled the toys as if they were rare glass ornaments, turning them carefully in his hands. He smiled with recognition at each item. I could tell that the gift meant a lot to him because his eyes got pretty moist.

"You'll notice there's not a single candy bar or bag of chips to be found," I pointed out. "Mom gave us specific instructions about that."

"Yup. Things are going to have to change," Watson said with a sigh. "They've put me on the Healthy Heart diet and I've taken a solemn oath that I will stick to it. Or else."

We both knew what "or else" meant. I quickly put that out of my mind and changed the subject to something more positive. "Mom said this will be good for all of us. It's our chance to learn healthy eating habits." I looked Watson in the eye and added, "And healthy work habits."

Watson held up both hands and grinned. "I know, I know. The hospital sent in an occupational counselor to talk to me. She told me that this warning shot across the bow wasn't just about eating right, but about living right."

"Which means?" I asked.

"It means cutting my work day in half," Watson replied. "Delegating more jobs to other people. And getting regular exercise."

"I can help you with that," I said confidently. "That's my specialty."

Watson chuckled once more. It was really good to hear him laugh. "Next thing I know, you'll have me jogging five miles a day and playing first base on Kristy's Krushers."

"Hmm . . ." I stroked my chin, exaggeratedly. "I see you more as a shortstop."

"Excuse me."

A nurse stuck her head in the room. A stethoscope dangled from her neck and she had a huge diver's watch strapped to her wrist. "Visiting hours are limited," she said crisply. "Mr. Brewer needs his rest."

"They're so *strict*," Watson whispered to me. "All I do around here is rest."

I leaned forward and gave him a big hug, which was kind of difficult because of all those wires attached to him. I was afraid I might unplug something.

"It's the best thing for you," I said. "Hurry up and get well, so you can come home."

Watson didn't let go right away. "That's all

I want, Kristy," he murmured, his voice thick with emotion. "To go home and be with my family."

Charlie and Sam were reading magazines in the waiting room when I came back.

"Ready to go?" Charlie asked.

I nodded. On our way out the door we ran into Mom. She had already gone home to check on the kids and was back to spend the evening (or as much time as the hospital staff would allow) with Watson.

"You look tired, Mom," I said. "You should get some rest, too."

She smiled wearily. "I plan to, honey. Just as soon as Watson comes home."

The boys went on ahead. I was about to follow when Mom took me by the hand. "I know this is difficult for everyone, but I just want you to know how much I appreciate all your help."

We said good-bye and promised to see each other in the morning before school.

Back at home, David Michael and Emily wanted a full report of my visit to the hospital. I described the room and the scary machines.

"Telemetry," David Michael told me. "That's what it's called when the patient is on a heart monitor."

I blinked in surprise. "Now how do you know that?"

David Michael shrugged. "I watch TV. When the ambulance comes, and the patient's heartbeat is really crazy, they put him on this stuff called a lidocaine drip. Then once they put him in the hospital and he's, um, stabilized, they put him on telemetry."

"What kind of a TV show tells you that?" I asked, running down my mental list of kids' programs.

He ticked off his list on the fingers of one hand. *"QRU. Call for Help. Rescue Rangers. Alert!* And *Emergency Room.* That's my favorite."

"Whatever happened to *Mister Rogers* and *Sesame Street*?" I asked.

David Michael made a face. "That's for babies. I'm in second grade."

"Sesame Street!" Emily clapped her hands together and headed for the living room. I guess she figured that, since we were talking about *Sesame Street*, it must be on television.

Nannie stepped into the hall from the kitchen and banged on an old frying pan with a wooden spoon. "Announcing the second seating for dinner in the Brewer dining room! This is your first and only call."

Sam heard the gong upstairs and made it to

the bottom of the stairs in just a few big leaps. Charlie met him at the dining room door and the two of them wrestled their way to the table.

"Aren't you eating?" I asked David Michael.

"No, I ate at the first seating." It tickled me to hear him use that formal restaurant talk. "Besides," he added, "I'm providing the entertainment."

"Let me guess," I said with a smile. "The rooster from *The Brementown Musicians*. Right?"

"Arr-er-arr-er-roo!" he answered, tucking his hands in his armpits and flapping his elbows like wings. Emily, who had been a little upset about not finding *Sesame Street* on the TV, caught on, and joined in.

Suddenly we had two roosters flapping and crowing at the tops of their lungs. And that's how the evening went. Charlie, Sam, and I ate our dinner and watched David Michael (with a little help from Emily Michelle) rehearse his part.

He was about to run through it for the third time when Mom called from the hospital. Watson wanted to say good night to all of us kids. I went first, then hurried to help Nannie with the dishes. While we cleaned the kitchen, we planned the next day's menu.

After the phone call was over, I marched the kids upstairs for their baths. Story time followed bath time. And by that time, I was totally exhausted. Too tired to do my homework. Too tired to call my friends. Too tired to even take a bath. I slipped on my pajamas, and fell into bed. What a long day!

Wednesday wasn't any easier. I was up early, helping Nannie. Charlie and Sam packed lunches while I made breakfast. We found out that Mom hadn't even come home from the hospital. I guess she'd fallen asleep in the chair beside Watson's bed and didn't wake up until morning. That threw everyone's schedules off, because she was supposed to take some of Watson's papers to his office after she waited with David Michael for the school bus.

We had a quick family huddle.

"I'll wait with David Michael," I said.

"I'll take the papers to Watson's office," Charlie volunteered. "Sam can ride with me."

"And I'll get Emily Michelle into her snow clothes," Nannie said.

"Right!"

Making plans for after school and the next few days was just as complicated.

"I've got BSC meetings today and Friday,"

I reminded everyone, "so I won't be able to watch the kids then."

"I've got my job," Sam added.

"Don't forget," Charlie said, "the seniors have our class trip Thursday."

"Class trip!" I gasped, thinking that now I'd be without transportation. "For how long?"

Charlie ruffled my hair good-naturedly. "Don't sweat it. It's just a day trip, but I won't be back until late."

Then Nannie went over her schedule. "We need to make sure everyone gets to the hospital to see Watson each day. Now Emily has a doctor's appointment on Thursday morning, and I've got a dentist appointment that afternoon. I did have a game scheduled Friday with my bowling league, but I could skip that. Someone needs to be here with the kids."

Coming up with a schedule that worked for all of us was mind boggling. It was the first time I really, truly understood what it must be like for Mom to run our household *and* hold down a full-time job.

Somehow we made it through the next few days without any disasters. Then on Friday, we got the good news.

"Watson is coming home Sunday," Mom announced after another long visit at the hospital. "The doctor says he's ready. He just has to take it very easy."

We decided that the whole family, including Karen and Andrew, would hold a welcome home party for him.

"It has to be low-key," Mom warned. "Just the family. No rowdy music." (She raised an eyebrow at Sam.) "Or loud TV." (She directed this at David Michael.) "Or wild group activities and games." (That comment was aimed at me.) "I want this party to be warm, welcoming and — dull."

I saluted. "One dull party, coming right up."

"Can't we at least decorate?" David Michael asked. "It won't be a party without decorations."

"Of course you can," Nannie said. "And we can make delicious food, too. It just can't be too fattening, or too sweet, and *no* cholesterol."

"That sounds like carrot and celery sticks with yogurt dip," I said, thinking of Stacey's and Dawn's healthful snacks.

Planning a dull party was more fun than we had thought it would be. I organized it (naturally) and gave everyone their assignments. Karen and Andrew were to make a *Welcome Home* banner for the front porch. Charlie and

Sam were in charge of picking dull music. I helped Nannie with the boring food. And David Michael was in charge of the low-key entertainment (his Brementown rooster, without the crowing).

On Sunday morning, Lisa brought Karen and Andrew to the house. They proudly unfurled their banner in the living room.

"How's this?" Karen asked.

The colors she had chosen were neon pink, lime green, and electric orange. From a distance, if you squinted to blur the image, the banner looked as if it had been hit with a huge scoop of rainbow sherbet.

"It's perfect," I said, giving her a hug.

We were all pretty huggy that morning. Emily Michelle had attached herself to my leg shortly after breakfast and wouldn't let go. Mom kept hugging and kissing everyone, declaring, "Isn't this wonderful? Watson's coming home!"

Charlie had been given the honor of bringing Watson home from the hospital. As a special treat, Mom had let him drive Watson's red sports car. Of course, she absolutely forbade him to drive anywhere near the speed limit. "Remember, Watson doesn't need any excitement. You drive slowly."

When the phone call came saying that they

were leaving the hospital, we all sprang into action. Nannie and I carried the hors d'oeuvres into the living room and put them on the coffee table. Sam slipped a CD into the player and turned the volume way down (a big first for my brother!). Mom changed Emily Michelle into her nicest dress. Any sooner and it would have been covered in yogurt and Claymate.

Then we lined up on the front porch and held hands — Mom, Emily, Nannie, David Michael, Karen, Andrew, Sam, and me. We waited under Karen's sherbet banner for Watson's return.

"There he is!" Andrew shouted as the sports car rounded the corner onto McLelland. "He's here!"

Charlie had taken Mom's warning about speeding seriously and was driving very slowly. It seemed to take hours for the car to creep down the street and finally turn into the drive. Mom hurried down the steps and met Watson at the car. We wanted to run after her and surround him but Nannie stopped us.

"Remember, low-key," she whispered. "Don't get him too excited."

The passenger door opened and Watson swung his feet onto the driveway. I was relieved to see him wearing regular clothes, instead of that ugly green hospital gown. It was obvious he was still weak, though. He had to hold on to Mom's and Charlie's arms to walk up the sidewalk. At the foot of the porch steps he let go and, clasping his hands together, looked up at us.

No one knew what to say. We just stood there with huge smiles on our faces. (I was grinning so hard, my cheeks hurt.) Watson took a long look at each one of us. His eyes brimmed with tears and his voice was a little shaky, but his words were filled with joy.

"You know, I've never seen anything so beautiful in my entire life."

Then he opened his arms. Nothing in the world could have stopped us from running to him then.

CHAPTER 7

"Nannie, Watson would like another apple juice," I said as I carried his dinner dishes into the kitchen. Nannie was busy loading the dishwasher. "Do we have any?"

Nannie pursed her lips. "We did. But I think the boys drank it all last night, watching TV. Can he have fruit punch?"

"Let me check the List."

The List of Forbidden Foods was posted on the refrigerator, right next to the week's menus and snacks.

Charlie had installed an intercom system to let Watson call almost anywhere in the house. There was a unit in the kitchen, in Mom and Watson's bedroom upstairs, and in the living room, aside from the master unit by Watson's bed in the library. He also wore a special device around his neck that he could use to call for help in case he fell while on his way to the bathroom.

The kitchen intercom clicked on and I heard Watson's voice say, "Kristy?"

I touched the talkback button. "Yes?"

"Cancel the juice, will you? I think I'm just going to take a little nap."

"It's a good thing he canceled the juice," I told Nannie as I checked the list. "Because fruit punch is a no-no. Too much sugar."

Nannie crossed to the kitchen bulletin board. "I'll put apple juice on Watson's shopping list and Sam can pick some up after school when he goes to work."

Mom had instituted a new system for us to follow. Before any of us left the house we were to check the bulletin board. The shopping list was there, and so were all of the daily schedules. I posted my baby-sitting jobs and sports activities, David Michael's play practice was written in, and Charlie and Sam listed their after-school activities. Nannie's bowling nights were clearly marked, and so were Mom's after-work meetings.

I studied the bulletin board and whistled. "Wow. We are one busy family."

Nannie smiled. "Busy, but organized. Your mom made sure of that. Otherwise she never would have felt comfortable returning to work."

Mom had taken some time off from her job to take care of Watson. She turned the library into a bedroom for him, so he wouldn't have to climb the stairs. She had picked the library because there he would be surrounded by the things he loved most — books.

. "Speaking of work," I said to Nannie, "Watson's office sent him another fax. But when I brought it to him, he didn't even look at it. He just told me to set it on his desk and he'd get to it."

"That's not like him," Nannie said, surprised. "I guess he's really following the doctor's orders to cut back."

"Not only that," I went on. "His secretary phoned at least three times yesterday and Watson wouldn't talk to her. He told me to tell her he didn't have time to talk, he was spending time with his family."

"And was he?" Nannie asked.

I shrugged. "Well, we were all sitting in the library with him. I was doing my homework and Emily was coloring. I think David Michael was going over his lines for the play. We weren't really talking to Watson."

"What was Watson doing?"

"Just watching us with a kind of teary-eyed

smile on his face. Which he does a lot lately."
I made sure the intercom in the kitchen was
off and whispered to Nannie, "It's kind of
weird, but he looks at me now like he's never
going to see me again. When I leave the room,
he says good-bye, as if I'm leaving forever."

Nannie put her arm around my shoulder.
"You have to understand, Kristy, Watson had
a tremendous scare. He really did think he
might not see any of us again. Now he wants
to make every second of his life count. I can
understand what he's feeling."

I guess I could, too, but it was kind of
strange for him do a flip-flop like that. One
second he was the king of the businessmen,
and the next he'd abandoned his work. All he
wanted to do was sit and stare at his family.

"Another fax came in," Charlie called from
the hall.

"Just put it on Watson's desk," I replied.

Charlie stuck his head in the kitchen. "Have
you seen his desk lately? It's piled high with
faxes, phone messages, and manila envelopes
that his office delivered."

Nannie and I looked at each other.

"Hmm," Nannie said. "I think it's time for
Elizabeth to talk to Watson about continuing
to work. Either he wants to work or he
doesn't."

"I think she should also have a talk with his office," I added.

That evening I was scheduled to baby-sit for Karen and Andrew, so I skipped dinner at my house. I hate to admit it, but I was relieved to spend an evening away from home. I had been working very hard, trying to help Mom and Nannie take care of the family and Watson. As good a patient as Watson tried to be, he still needed people to bring him things. He also really wanted company. I sat in the library as much as I could, but I was beginning to go a little stir-crazy.

Seth, Karen's and Andrew's stepfather, picked me up at six and drove me to their house. He was genuinely concerned about Watson. I asked him how Karen and Andrew were doing.

"Andrew is his normal loveable self," Seth replied. "But Karen is being a little difficult at the moment."

"Difficult? How?"

"You'll see soon enough." He pulled the car into the drive of the little house. (Karen calls her mom's house the little house and our house the big house. Now I'm starting to do it.)

"There's Karen," Seth said.

She was standing in the living room, staring

80

out the picture window. Karen wore her pink glasses (she also has blue ones that she wears for reading) and her blonde hair was pulled into pigtails.

I waved at her. Usually Karen runs to greet me with a sunny smile. Today all she offered was a scowl.

"Is that what you mean?" I asked as I followed Seth up the walk to the front door.

"Yup. Karen's mad, and she's standing at the window so the whole world will know it."

Before I could ask what she was mad about, the front door swung open and Seth's dog, Midgie, galloped out to greet us. Andrew was right behind her.

"Kristy, wait till you see what I built," he cried. Midgie ran circles around us, barking hello. I kept an eye on the door, waiting for Karen to appear.

She didn't.

"I built a castle with my Legos. Come see." Andrew pulled me up the front steps and into the rec room.

Seth, who was right behind us, continued upstairs. "I'll just tell Lisa you're here."

Andrew had built his castle in the middle of the room. He'd really worked hard on it, too. It had two tall towers and even a drawbridge across a moat made out of blue construction paper. He'd combined several toy sets so that small Lego knights and horses were surrounded by large wooden cows and sheep.

"There's even a magical wizard inside," Andrew said, beaming proudly. "And I did the whole thing myself."

"You did not," Karen said, marching across the room to the couch and pointing. "I made the moat and the bushes."

"You did a great job, Karen," I said, trying to ease her out of her very grumpy mood. "They make Andrew's castle look totally real."

Karen was in no mood for compliments. She flopped onto the couch and sat with her arms folded firmly across her chest. "Hmmph."

"Okay, kids, we're leaving now," Lisa said, sticking her head in the door. She gave me a big smile. "Hi, Kristy. How are you?"

"A little fried," I admitted. "It feels nice to get away from home a bit. Things are pretty crazy right now."

"Well, if you do not like it," Karen said, "trade places with me. I will stay at the big house with Daddy."

Lisa sighed loudly. "Karen, we've gone over and over that. The decision is final."

I was starting to catch a glimmer of what

was behind Karen's bad mood. Obviously it had something to do with wanting to stay with Watson.

"It's not fair," Karen grumbled, stubbornly puffing out her lower lip.

Lisa ignored Karen and turned back to me. "Kristy, I've left the phone number of where we'll be on the fridge. Dinner is in the plastic container on the counter. Just pop it into the microwave for five minutes."

Seth brought Lisa her coat. "Come on, honey. We'd better hurry or we'll be late."

" 'Bye, kids," Lisa called. "Have fun with Kristy. And Karen?" She gave Karen a stern look. "You behave yourself."

Karen rolled her eyes but said nothing. She waited until the front door shut and Seth and Lisa were safely out of the driveway. Then she let loose.

"I'm mad," Karen said, punching one of the couch cushions. "Mommy won't let me go to the big house to see Daddy."

"That's not true, Karen. She brought you and Andrew over two days ago."

"For fifteen minutes." Karen threw the couch cushion on the floor. "That's not enough time for anything. Besides, I don't want to go *visit* Daddy, I want to *stay* with him."

"You *will* stay with him," I told her. "Next month. But this month is your mom's month."

The kids used to stay with Watson every other weekend, but Karen and Andrew wanted to spend more time with their dad, so Watson and Lisa agreed on an every-other-month system for the kids.

"They should switch months," Karen cried. "Daddy is sick and we should be with him."

Andrew, who'd been quietly moving his knights and wizards around the castle, chimed in. "Daddy needs us. We can help him feel better."

I could see that Karen was hurting and my heart went out to her. "Karen, I know this is tough for you, but if they start switching months, then everything will get confused. Your mom and Seth have arranged their schedules for the year. Your dad and my mom have planned family vacations around your visits. It would just be too confusing."

Karen's chin was starting to quiver. "But I want to be with my daddy!"

I wrapped my arms around my stepsister and squeezed her tight. "Don't cry, Karen. Before you know it, February will be here and we'll all be together at the big house."

The rest of the evening was pretty subdued. Andrew played with his castle, we ate lasagna — and Karen sulked. I couldn't blame her. But let's face it, a whole evening with a grumpy seven-year-old is no fun.

CHAPTER 8

Thursday

Five kids! Mrs. Marshall wanted me to baby-sit for five kids! I didn't have the nerve to tell her that even at my own house, four kids is the absolute limit before we get another sitter. In fact, that's our club rule. Instead, I acted like everything was fine. Boy, was I wrong! And boy, am I glad Jessi came to the rescue.

It seemed as though Mrs. Marshall was starting to make a habit of surprising my friends in the BSC. First Dawn, and then Mallory. Her excuse was the same both times.

"Mrs. Phillips and I have our jazzercise class this afternoon, so I told her to leave her kids here and we'd drive together," Mrs. Marshall explained, looping her gym bag over her shoulder. "There's bologna and ham and sliced cheese in the refrigerator. Just throw together some sandwiches for the kids and toss a few potato chips and some apple slices on their plates. That should hold them."

The minute Mrs. Marshall and Mrs. Phillips left, five kids appeared at the top of the stairs. Nina was in tears. "It was my turn to jump on the bed, and Moira took it."

"I'm older," Moira, who had been briefly introduced to Mallory, explained. "The oldest gets to go first."

"Jumping on the bed!" Mallory cried. "Nobody gets to go first. We don't jump on the bed."

"We always jump on the bed at our house," Bryant said as he slid down the bannister. Mallory caught him at the bottom of the rail.

"And it's not a good idea to do that, either,"

Mallory said, pulling him off the railing and setting him firmly on the floor.

"Jump! I jump, too," Eleanor cried, hopping in place at the top of the stairs.

"Be careful, Eleanor!" Mallory wove her way between Moira and her three-year-old brother Tyler, and hurried to take Eleanor's hand. "Let's all go downstairs, where it's safe and I can watch you."

"No!" Eleanor cried. "I jump."

She jerked her hand away and Mallory lost her balance. She fell against the stair railing, bumping into Tyler.

Tyler, his eyes two big surprised circles, tumbled in a perfect backward somersault to the bottom of the stairs. His body hit the soft carpet but he banged his lip against the bottom step.

Then everything went crazy. Tyler cried out in pain, and his lip started to bleed. The blood frightened everyone, including Mal. Eleanor instantly burst into tears. "Mommy! I want my mommy!"

"I'll go find her," Bryant said, heading for the front door.

Mallory, who had rushed to Tyler's side, didn't know which way to turn. Eleanor was crying at the top of the stairs, and Mal was worried she might pull a Tyler, too, and tumble down.

Then Moira added to the commotion by punching Mal on the shoulder. "You hurt my brother," she said. "You pushed him down the stairs."

Mal was overwhelmed by the noise, the crying, and the sheer number of kids she had to deal with. She took a deep breath and tried to take charge.

"Bryant, you stay right here!" Mallory ordered as she scooped Tyler into her arms. "Nina, watch Eleanor. I'm taking Tyler to the kitchen. Moira, come with me and help your brother."

Mallory grabbed a clean kitchen towel from the drawer and set Tyler on the counter beside the sink. She ran the towel under cool water and pressed it against his lip.

Moira still wasn't helping. "He's really bleeding!" she said tearfully. "Look at all that blood."

Mallory told me later that she wanted to cry herself. It was just too much to handle. She forced herself to stay calm and spoke to Moira and Tyler the way her mom would have talked to her.

"Moira, I know it looks scary," Mal said as

she applied pressure to Tyler's lip. "But it's not as bad as it seems. See? It's just a little cut. Tyler will be fine in no time."

By now Tyler had stopped crying and was making little hiccuping sounds. "You are such a brave boy," Mal said, giving him a hug. "Moira and I are so proud of you. Right, Moira?"

Moira, who looked pretty pale herself, nodded. "He's a good brother."

Mal kept talking. It seemed to keep the chaos under control. "Let's see. When I cut my lip, Mom always puts something cold on it. I'll just carry Tyler over to the refrigerator and we'll look for an ice cube."

Mal balanced Tyler on her hip with one hand and swung open the freezer door with the other. She spotted a box of Popsicles.

"Perfect!" Mal cried. "A Popsicle is cold and it tastes good. Tyler, would you like a cherry Popsicle?"

Tyler, tears still streaking down his cheeks, nodded solemnly.

Instantly Moira was at Mal's side. "I want a Popsicle, too."

Bryant, who had taken his coat off, heard the word Popsicle and ran into the kitchen. "Not fair. They get Popsicles."

Mal checked the box. There were only four

Popsicles in the box and five kids. She knew the chances of one of them not wanting a Popsicle were slim. Mal had to think fast. She decided to make a phone call.

"I have an idea. I'm going to put Tyler in a chair at the table with his special hurt-lip Popsicle. If you and Moira sit by your brother, I'll make a quick phone call to my friend and she can bring us some more Popsicles. That way everyone can have one."

Moira and Bryant did as they were told, but Mal could tell they didn't quite believe what she had said. Once the kids were seated at the table, Mal raced into the hall to check on the Marshall kids. "Nina? Eleanor? Where are you two?"

Nina poked her head out of the bathroom. "We're in here, washing our dollies' hair."

The girls had pulled two chairs up to the bathroom sink, which was filled to the brim with water. Floating in the middle were two fully clothed dolls.

"Oh, brother," Mallory moaned. "I need help. Now!"

She hurried to the phone in the kitchen and called Jessi. Luckily for Mal, Jessi was home.

"Jessi, this is an emergency," Mal exclaimed. "I need you to come help me, quick."

"What's happened? Is somebody hurt?"

Mal quickly explained that she was baby-sitting for five kids and that already Tyler had split his lip. Mallory could barely catch her breath as she talked. It all rattled out of her in one, long sentence. "Everyone was crying and blood was everywhere, and I tried to get it to stop so I gave him a Popsicle, and now all the kids want Popsicles and I don't have enough, and I think Nina and Eleanor are flooding the bathroom — "

"Mal!" Jessi cut in. "Calm down. It's going to be okay. I'll be right over. I'll bring Popsicles and any other treats I can find."

"Oh, thank you, thank you, thank you!" Mal said gratefully.

Mal hung up the phone and hurried back to check on Eleanor and Nina. The dolls were still floating in the sink, but now there was water all over the floor.

"Time to dry the dollies," Mal said, handing each girl a towel and then pulling the plug in the sink. "If you don't, they might catch cold."

"Oh, poor dolly," Nina said, gently cradling hers in the towel. "We don't want you to get sick."

Eleanor watched her sister and imitated her. "Poor dolly."

"Why don't you girls bring your dolls into the kitchen?" Mallory suggested. "Jessi's coming over and bringing us some treats."

Mallory herded the girls into the kitchen and then slumped into a chair.

Jessi lives two blocks away, so she made it to the Marshalls' house in less than five minutes. She arrived just in the nick of time, too. Tyler had finished his Popsicle and was smearing his sticky hands on Moira's shoulder.

"Ew! Gross!" she cried. "Tyler's getting red goo all over me."

"Never fear, Jessi's here." Jessi announced as she entered the kitchen. She held a box of Fruit Pops in one hand and a bag of Chee·tos in the other. "Now which one of you split his lip?"

Tyler raised his hand and Mallory introduced the rest of the kids. "Their mom and Mrs. Marshall are taking jazzercize classes together."

"Are there only five kids here?" Jessi asked.

"Yes, why?" said Mallory.

"Because I had to step over a pile of about ten coats in the front hall."

"What?" Mal sprang to her feet. "Who did that?"

Bryant grinned. "Me. I was making a fort."

"Oh, great." Mal shook her head. "It's been like this ever since their moms left. The bathroom is flooded, there's blood all over the sink and cherry Popsicle juice all over the kids. I'm afraid to look at the carpet, where Tyler's lip dripped."

"Why don't we take turns cleaning?" Jessi said as she passed out Popsicles to the rest of the children. "One of us can watch the kids while the other does the bathroom. Then we can switch, and clean the kitchen and front hall."

"Sounds like a good plan to me," Mal said. She smiled gratefully at Jessi. "Boy, am I glad you're here. I think I was about to lose it."

"What are best friends for?" Jessi said, doing a springy *jeté*. "You sit right there, while I start on that bathroom floor."

Mal cleaned Tyler up while the rest of the kids ate their Popsicles. This time she managed to give them each a napkin.

Everything went smoothly for the next hour and a half as Mal and Jessi took turns cleaning and sitting. Then, moments before it was time for the moms to return, Mallory suddenly cried out, "Oh, no!"

"What?" Jessi ran into the den, where the kids were playing a board game. "What happened? Did somebody else get hurt?"

"Dinner!" Mallory cried, slapping herself on the side of her head. "I forgot to fix them dinner."

Jessi and Mallory stared at each other. Finally Jessi said, "They had dinner. Chee·tos and popsicles."

"That's not dinner," Mallory stammered. "That — that's . . ."

"Emergency dinner," Jessi said firmly. "You had a crisis and the kids ate what would make them happy. It wasn't exactly the most nutritious meal on the planet, but they had fruit juice and cheese. That's not so terrible."

When Mrs. Marshall and Mrs. Phillips came home, they were surprised to find Jessi there. Mallory explained, in great detail, what had happened over the past two and a half hours. "Lucky for me, Jessi was able to come help," Mallory said. "Or the house would be a mess."

"Thanks for helping, Jessi," Mrs. Marshall said as she opened her wallet. "But I hope you don't expect to be paid for it. I only hired one sitter."

Mallory was so stunned, she couldn't say a word. She looked at Jessi, who said slowly, "I guess I understand, Mrs. Marshall. I only came over because Mallory really needed help."

Mal and Jessi left the house in shock. They walked half a block, then Mallory turned to Jessi. "I can't believe it," she blurted out. "Mrs. Marshall never told me that I would be taking care of five kids. But she expected me to watch them. I truly needed your help. And then she refused to pay you for it. That really makes me mad!"

Jessi felt the same way. "Five kids, especially when they're so little — that's just too much for one sitter to handle. We need to talk to Kristy about this."

"I'll call her tonight," Mallory said, glancing back at the Marshall house. "We can't let this happen again."

When Mal called me that night, we agreed to talk about it at the next BSC meeting. Then I wrote this note to myself on my pad:

Friday: Top Priority — Mrs. Marshall and too many kids !!!

Oh, by the way, Mallory split her pay with Jessi.

CHAPTER 9

"Listen up, everyone." Watson tapped the side of his crystal water glass with his spoon. "I have an important announcement to make."

We were gathered in our formal dining room for the first sit-down family dinner since Watson's return from the hospital. Mom had made a big event of it, ordering flowers and making sure we all wore our nicest clothes. I was in a dress, believe it or not, and Charlie, Sam, and even David Michael sported ties. Emily Michelle looked like a fancy box of candy in her pink satin lace dress and bows. Nannie wore her best linen pants suit and Mom looked especially beautiful in the dress she wore on her first date with Watson. All in all, I'd have to say the Brewer/Thomas family looked pretty darn good.

"First of all, I'd like to compliment the chef."

Watson raised his glass to Nannie and we followed suit.

"To the chef!"

"Now, I'd like to tell you, my wonderful family, how much you mean to me and just how happy I am to be able to stand here and look at your beaming faces." He raised his glass to the family. "Here's looking at you, kids!"

"To us!" we cried.

David Michael took that as his cue. "I'd like to propose a toast to Shannon, Boo-Boo, Goldfishie, and Crystal Light the second."

Watson grinned and raised his glass. "To the Brewer Zoo."

"To the zoo!" we chorused.

Mom stood up. "Now I'd like to make a toast to my husband. Welcome home, Watson."

"Hooray for Watson!" David Michael led the cheering.

Emily Michelle loved that. She clapped her hands together.

Watson and the rest of us lifted our water glasses to Emily Michelle. "To Emily."

Then Watson cleared his throat. "I made an important decision today that will affect all of us."

"We're not moving, are we?" David Michael

suddenly paled. "I have to do my play. The rooster is a really important part."

Watson chuckled. "Don't worry, we're not moving. I like it here. In fact, I like it so much that I've decided to stay home."

"Permanently?" I blinked in surprise. "You mean, quit your job?"

"Not exactly," Watson explained. "I would just turn the business over to one of the vice-presidents. She can manage the day-to-day affairs and, if she needs an executive decision, she can contact me here. But for now, I want to be a stay-at-home dad."

"Mr. Mom," I whispered to Charlie.

Watson heard me and chuckled. "Mr. Mom. Exactly."

Mom scooted back her chair and planted a kiss on the top of Watson's bald head. "I'm all for it. You'll get plenty of rest and we'll be able to spend more time with you."

Watson held up one hand. "Now, I'm not just going to sit around the house. I plan to cook, and clean, and make sure you all get dressed and off to school."

"Will you even pack our lunches?" David Michael asked.

"Of course," Watson said. "I'm going to do everything that Nannie's had to do."

I looked at Nannie for her reaction. She was

staring at her plate intently. I wondered if she'd even heard his announcement.

Nannie must have read my mind, because she raised her head and said, "Watson, I'm so happy for you."

Eventually we finished dinner, but not before David Michael had treated us to his rendition of the entire play (including all of the parts) of *The Brementown Musicians*.

Watson said he was going to be a stay-at-home dad and that's what he became. Instantly. When I got up the next morning, Watson was already in the kitchen cooking breakfast. He was wearing a red-and-white striped apron and a white chef's hat.

"Pull up a chair, ma'am, and I'll take your order." Watson gestured toward the big kitchen table. "We have bacon and eggs, yogurt and fruit, biscuits and grits, pancakes. You name it, we make it."

I decided to keep it simple. "I'll just have a bowl of cereal."

"Really? Is that all?" Watson looked genuinely disappointed.

"Sorry, but that's about all I can handle." I poured myself a glass of orange juice from the pitcher on the table.

"Well," he said with a grin, "maybe Emily will go for some pancakes."

I didn't have the heart to break it to him that Emily was on a Cocoa Puffs-only kick. I figured he'd find out soon enough. "Speaking of Emily," I said, "should I wake her up?"

"Nope, I've already done that," Watson replied. "I got her dressed, and Nannie is upstairs combing her hair. They should be down any minute."

Sam stuck his head in the kitchen door. "How're my pancakes coming?"

"They're warming in the oven." Watson opened the oven door and pulled out a plate covered with another plate. "Did you get your science project loaded into Charlie's car?"

"Yeah," Sam replied. "I'm just going to wash my hands and I'll be right back."

"Careful of the bathroom floor," Watson called after him. "I just mopped it and it may be a little slick."

I nearly choked on my orange juice. "You washed the bathroom floor? This morning?"

"Sure. It was a cinch." Watson flipped his pancake spatula in the air. "I got up early to talk to your mom and I noticed some muddy footprints in there, so I found the mop and scrubbed it."

"Wow," I said, shaking my head. "I'm impressed."

I really was, too. By the end of the week,

Watson was not only Mr. Mom, he had become Super-Mom. He managed to get everyone up, dressed, fed and off to school without too many problems. (He mixed up everyone's lunches one day and put Emily Michelle's dress on her backward another.) In the evenings he cooked us dinner. We had Watson's special Thai stir-fry and steamed rice on Monday, Watson's low-fat crock-pot chili on Tuesday, and Watson's baked chicken breasts (no skin) on Wednesday. By Thursday, Nannie insisted that he take a break.

"You're supposed to be taking it easy, remember?" she said. "At the rate you're going, you'll have another heart attack. I'll come in and find you passed out with your nose in the fondue pot."

Watson begrudgingly let Nannie cook dinner on Thursday, but by Friday he'd regained his position in the kitchen. "We're having Watson's grilled halibut steaks with a squeeze of lemon and herbs, accompanied by a steamed vegetable medley."

Nannie, who is usually a lot of fun to be around, seemed to be getting quieter and quieter. By the end of the week, she was eating her meals in silence.

I noticed that when she wasn't looking after Emily Michelle, she pretty much stayed in her room. I wondered if she was getting sick.

"I've worried about that myself," Mom said, when I mentioned my concern to her. "Nannie seems to be pretty listless. Usually she's a pistol around the house, running up and down those stairs and ordering everyone about. Last night, I barely saw her. When she did come out of her room, it was just to get a glass of milk and a magazine."

"Maybe we should tell her to go to the doctor." After our scare with Watson, I was extra concerned about everyone's health.

Mom patted me on the arm. "I'll talk to Nannie about it. But don't worry, Kristy. Nannie's as healthy as a horse. She'll outlive us all."

Hoping to make myself stop worrying, I poked my head into her room that night. "Hi, Nannie. How's it going?"

Nannie was sitting in the wingback chair in the corner of her room, reading. She peered at me over top of her glasses. "It's going just fine. What are you up to?"

I shrugged. "I just wanted to see if you were feeling okay. We're having a hot game of Monopoly downstairs and we're wondering when you might join us."

"Oh, you kids don't need me to play with you," she said. "You've got Watson."

"Yes, but . . ." I stepped into the room and whispered, "He's a terrible player. Don't ever let him be the banker. He gets it all mixed up."

Nannie set her book on the shelf beside her. "Well, maybe I could manage one good game of Monopoly before bed. But only if you're the banker."

"It's a deal," I said, throwing open her bedroom door.

Arr-er-arr-er-roo! The sound of a rooster crowing floated up the stairs.

"Gee, I wonder who that could be?" I joked.

"Isn't that David Michael Thomas?" Nannie replied. "Famous young actor and star of *The Brementown Musicians*?"

"In our house?" I said in mock surprise. "Come on, let's go ask him for his autograph."

"Race you," Nannie shouted. "Last one to the library is a rotten egg!"

She burned past me so fast I didn't realize what was happening. I put my hands on my hips and shouted, "Not fair. You had a head start."

Nannie answered me with a wild laugh as she headed down the stairs.

"Mom was right," I told my reflection in the hall mirror. "Nannie's going to outrun and outlive us all!"

CHAPTER 10

I was amazed. In a short time, Watson had changed from Mr. Hot Shot Executive, driving a snappy red sports car and making deals on his car phone, to plain old Mr. Mom, hauling kids and pets and groceries everywhere in the van. As his health improved he took over driving David Michael to play rehearsals and Emily Michelle to the playground. He even chauffeured me to a BSC meeting.

"I told Charlie he could take the afternoon off," Watson said, as he slid open the van door. "Emily Michelle and I thought we'd take a little drive. On the way we can pick up David Michael and maybe cruise around your old neighborhood while you have your meeting."

I hopped in the van and we drove off down McLelland Street. "Watson, I have to admit, when you first said you wanted to become a stay-at-home dad, I didn't think you'd be able to pull it off."

"So what do you think now?" he asked me.

"You're doing a terrific job," I said with a grin.

Watson shrugged. "I figured, if I could run a multi-national corporation with six hundred employees, I should be able to manage a household of ten."

"Two, three, four, ten!" Emily Michelle piped up from the back seat.

"Good counting, Emily," Watson said, proudly. "She's starting to put more and more words together. Pretty soon she'll go from being a two-year-old to a first-grader."

"To starring in plays like David Michael," I added.

"Kids grow up so fast." Watson's eyes became misty. "Before you know it, they're out the door and on their own."

Being Mr. Mom had helped Watson move past his super-emotional phase, but every now and then he had a mushy moment. This was one of them.

While I was at my BSC meeting, Watson and the kids picked up a pizza from Pizza Express. He ordered a garden salad for himself. I love pizza, and I like everything on it (especially anchovies).

Emily Michelle and David Michael also adore pizza and insisted on holding the warm carton on their laps as we drove home. (It wasn't really on Emily's lap because she was in her car seat, but she held onto a corner.)

Unfortunately, Nannie hadn't known about the pizza. When we walked in the door, the dinner table was set and a big platter of Nannie's pasta primavera was already on the table.

"I wish I'd known you were bringing home a pizza," she said, an extremely tight smile on her face.

"I wish you'd told me that you were cooking dinner," Watson replied, just as stiffly.

Nannie didn't flinch. "I always cook dinner. I've been doing it for as long as I've been living here."

Things were starting to sound tense so I said, "Why don't we just freeze the pizza? We can have it tomorrow night."

That might have been a good solution if Emily Michelle and David Michael hadn't had their hearts set on pizza.

"No, you can't," David Michael cried, unaware of what was going on between Watson and Nannie. "We want pizza."

Something in Nannie snapped. "Then I'll just freeze my dinner," she said, throwing up her hands in frustration. "Of course, you

107

really can't freeze pasta, so I guess instead I'll just give it to the cat, or — "

"Hold your horses," Watson cut in. "I can't eat pizza, but I do love pasta. And it's on my diet plan. Why don't we give the kids pizza, and the grown-ups can have pasta?"

"Great idea!" I said in an extra cheery voice. I didn't know whether I was included in the grown-up or the kid count, but I was fully prepared to eat both meals if it would make everyone happy.

After that evening, Nannie and Watson made sure they checked with each other before planning dinner. In fact, things settled into a nice routine at our house, so that by the end of the month, I could hardly remember what it had been like when Watson worked full-time.

That's why it took me, and everyone in my family, by complete surprise when Nannie made her big announcement.

It was on a Thursday evening. We had gathered in the den to watch a little TV and play chess (Watson was trying to teach it to David Michael and me). Everyone thought Nannie had gone to her room for the night, but suddenly she appeared with a handful of brochures. She laid them on the table and told us her news.

"I've rented an apartment," she said with a smile.

This floored Mom. "An apartment? What on earth for?"

"To live in," Nannie said patiently.

"I realize that," my mother continued. "But why do you want to move?"

Nannie folded her hands in her lap. "I've been thinking about this for some time," she said carefully. "I really feel that I need my own place. Where I can come and go as I please."

"But you can do that here," I said.

"I know." Nannie touched me affectionately on the cheek. "But it's not the same as having your very own place. And the one I've found is lovely. It's in the Waterford Gardens apartment complex just outside Stoneybrook."

"You're moving?" The reality of what Nannie was saying suddenly hit David Michael hard. "But you can't. We'll miss you."

"Oh, fiddle!" Nannie waved her hand in the air. "You won't even notice that I'm gone. Besides, I'll be over here visiting all the time. And I'll expect you to come see me."

"But how can I?" David Michael asked. "You just said your new apartment is outside Stoneybrook. And I'm not allowed to ride my bike farther than two blocks."

"Well, Charlie or your mom or Watson can

bring you over to see me." David Michael didn't like that answer, so Nannie tried another tack. "Or when you want to see me, you can just call and I'll drive over in the Pink Clinker and pick you up myself."

"Nannie bye-bye?" Emily Michelle said, her lower lip quivering. "No!" She ran across the room, hurled herself into Nannie's arms, and burst into tears.

Nannie squeezed her tight and murmured, "Emily, Emily, I'm not going away. I'll still be here for you."

I wanted to do what Emily Michelle had done and throw myself into Nannie's arms. But, of course, I didn't. I just sat like a big lump. I stared at her apartment brochures, trying to think of something encouraging to say.

Finally I murmured, "If that's what makes you happy, Nannie, then I'm glad for you."

"Yes," Mom echoed. "If this is really and truly what you want to do, then we're all happy for you."

She sounded about as convincing as I did. Because we *weren't* happy. We were miserable.

Especially on moving day, which as it turned out came only two days later. I looked after the kids while Charlie and Sam loaded Nannie's belongings into a U-Haul truck.

" 'Bye, Nannie rocker." Emily Michelle waved forlornly as the worn red velvet rocker was carried down the stairs and stowed into the truck. This was the chair that Nannie had often used to rock Emily Michelle to sleep. It gave me a weird feeling to see it go.

" 'Bye, magic trunk," David Michael said as the boys carried out Nannie's big steamer trunk. It really was magical. Nannie kept all kinds of wonderful things in it — old letters, pictures, and just neat odds and ends that she'd saved over the years. Once in a while, on rainy days or long winter nights, Nannie would open the trunk and let us explore it. It was like taking a trip through time, because everything we pulled out would prompt a story from when Nannie was a girl.

" 'Bye, trunk," I echoed David Michael.

Next went Nannie's bed, and matching dresser and vanity. Then Nannie's standing mirror that Karen and the kids had used so many times when they played dress-up. I could feel my heart breaking.

After the furniture and suitcases were loaded into the van, Nannie hugged and kissed us. Then she climbed into the front seat of the truck with Charlie and Sam. They drove away, and she was gone — just like that.

Emily Michelle knew something terrible had

happened. She cried twenty minutes after Nannie left. Nothing any of us did could console her. Finally, Mom suggested we just pile in the car and go over to Nannie's new apartment.

That made Emily feel a little better, and the car ride over actually lulled her to sleep. When we reached the apartment, the boys were still unloading furniture.

"Nannie, we're not going to stay long," Mom explained, as we carried the sleeping Emily to the apartment building. "Emily Michelle was so upset that we promised we'd follow you. So now that we're here, why don't you give us a tour of your new place?"

Waterford Gardens was, as Nannie put it, "utterly charming." Built in 1905, the building had been completely remodeled, with brand-new kitchens, floors, and everything. Each apartment had a small living room, a kitchen, one bedroom, and a bath. Sliding doors led out to a courtyard. That's what made it so charming. Even in the middle of winter, it looked like an English country garden with little rock paths and white trellises and pretty wrought iron benches scattered throughout.

"The garden is what sold me on the place," Nannie said as she led us back through her apartment. "I knew I could be happy if I had a pleasant place to drink my coffee in the morning."

"How many buildings did you look at?" I asked, picking up the groggy Emily and following everyone out to the car.

"Oh, half a dozen," Nannie replied.

Mom pursed her lips. "I didn't even know you were looking. I wish you had told me."

"You had your hands full," Nannie said. "I didn't want to bother you."

Mom paused beside the car and studied Nannie's face. "It's not too late to change your mind, you know. Most of your furniture is still in the truck."

Nannie hesitated just long enough to make me think she might change her mind. But then she chuckled and gave Mom and Emily a hug. "I'll be just fine here. Now you get back home. You have two more kids coming to join you soon."

"Two more kids?" Mom asked, knitting her brow.

"Karen and Andrew," Nannie reminded her. "Tomorrow is the start of their month at the big house."

"Oh gosh," Mom replied, "I forgot all about that."

"Karen hasn't," I assured her. "I think she's had her bags packed since Watson went into the hospital."

Nannie made a shooing motion with her hands. "Off you go. Watson's going to need your help making the house ready."

We drove off, leaving Nannie waving from the lawn of her new home.

On the drive back, Mom and I talked about how nice the gardens were and how clean and open the apartment seemed to be. What we didn't talk about was how much we were going to miss Nannie. Or how Emily Michelle was going to deal with her beloved grandmother's being gone. Someday, after we'd grown used to Nannie's absence, we'd probably be able to talk about it. But not now. It hurt too much.

CHAPTER 11

Tuesday

Claud and I both went to the Marshalls' for the Tuesday sitting job and, sure enough, five kids were there.

Talk about emberessing. Mrs. Marshall wasn't expekting two sitters.

And boy, was everything weird. Mrs. Marshall, who is usually so nice, was totally cold.

A reel ice cube. Burrrrrr!

It started from the moment she answered the door...

Mrs. Marshall had called for a sitter during the Friday BSC meeting. Stacey took the job, but the call set off a big discussion. Dawn talked about her job at the Marshalls', where she'd expected to care for two kids and wound up watching five. She said nothing terrible had happened but it might have. Then Mallory retold her horrible experience, when Tyler had tumbled down the stairs and cut his lip. Mal and Jessi emphasized the fact that two sitters were needed for that many kids (especially since three of the children were four and under). Not to mention our club rule about two sitters being required for more than four kids.

That's when I made my (as Watson would say) *executive* decision. "I think we should definitely send two sitters," I announced.

"But what if it's only the Marshall kids?" Mary Anne pointed out.

"Then the second sitter can leave," I replied. "But we don't want Stacey to have to care for five kids. It's just not safe."

Mallory nodded. "I agree with Kristy. Tyler fell down the stairs and only cut his lip, but something far worse could have happened. Watching those kids was really tough."

"Then it's official." I banged my pencil like a gavel on Claudia's desk. "Two sitters will go to the Marshalls' house Tuesday."

Claudia was nervous about going with Stacey. On the way to the Marshalls', she worried that we might have overreacted, but when Moira Phillips answered the door, Claud and Stacey knew we had made the right decision.

"Hello, Stacey," Mrs. Marshall called from the upstairs bedroom. "Come on in. I'm just grabbing my jazzercise shoes."

Stacey and Claud stepped into the foyer.

"Uh, Mrs. Marshall?" Stacey called up the stairs. "I brought Claudia along with me."

"That's fine," Mrs. Marshall said, hurrying down the stairs. "Hi, Claudia. How are you?"

Claudia and Stacey exchanged glances. Then Stacey continued, "I brought her along to be a second sitter."

Mrs. Marshall paused with her arm halfway in her coat. "You mean you both want to be paid?"

Claud and Stacey nodded.

"But I can't pay two sitters. I only asked for one."

"Yes, but there are five kids here," Stacey said.

"Is that a problem?" Mrs. Marshall's voice had taken on an irritated edge.

"Yes, I think it is," Stacey replied. "I can't responsibly care for five children. Especially when they're so little. It's just not safe."

Mrs. Marshall was still standing with her coat half on. "I won't pay for two sitters," she said with a shrug, "and that's that."

Stacey didn't even look at Claudia for support this time. She just stared Mrs. Marshall straight in the eye. "Then I'm sorry, Mrs. Marshall, but I won't be able to baby-sit for you today."

Claudia hurried to open the door. She told me later that she could feel her face turning bright red. And she knew Stacey must be feeling the same way.

"Wait a minute!" Mrs. Marshall called, as Stacey started to leave. "What about my dance class?"

"I'm sorry, Mrs. Marshall," Stacey mumbled, no longer able to look at her. "But I have to leave."

Once out on the street, Claudia and Stacey speedwalked to the corner without looking back. The minute they turned the corner, Stacey threw herself into a bank of snow and covered her face with her mittened hands. "I never want to go through that again," she exclaimed. "That was just *awful*."

"Did you see the look on Mrs. Marshall's face?" Claudia cried. "She was furious!"

"First my ears burned, then my whole face

turned red, then I saw little spots in front of my eyes," Stacey said, reliving the embarrassing experience.

"You sounded totally together," Claudia said. "I was impressed. Big time."

"I felt like such a jerk." Stacey wiggled her hands and shook her head. "Ew! Ick, ick, *ick*!" Suddenly Stacey stopped and stared wide-eyed at Claudia. "What if Mrs. Marshall hates us? I'll never be able to face her again."

"She can't hate us," Claudia replied. "We were only trying to be responsible baby-sitters. Besides, it's a club rule — two sitters for more than four kids."

"I hope Mrs. Marshall understands that." Stacey slushed her boots through the snow. "I'd hate to have her permanently angry with us and then tell other clients what happened."

"I think this is something the whole club should deal with," Claudia said, pulling Stacey to her feet. "Let's talk to Kristy and the others, and see what we should do."

The next afternoon, I arrived at Claudia's house a few minutes early, so Stacey and Claud filled me in on what had happened.

"This is really serious," I said.

I called the meeting to order at exactly five-thirty. Then Stacey and Claudia told their story, including every detail they could re-

119

member: Mrs. Marshall with her coat half on, looking shocked and angry; the five children fighting over a toy in the background; the way Claudia's and Stacey's faces felt as they walked out the door.

"I'm glad it was you and not me," Mary Anne said. "I probably would have broken down in tears."

"You were really brave," Mallory told Stacey, her voice full of admiration. "When I baby-sat, I didn't have the nerve to insist that Jessi be paid. I wimped out."

"I don't blame you," Claudia said. "I was a wimp, too. I let Stacey do all the talking. The only thing I did was open the door and run."

"You guys, maybe we should have called Mrs. Marshall first and told her we were sending two sitters," Dawn said thoughtfully. "I mean, she might have gone for it if she had known ahead of time."

I winced and nodded. "You're right. We should have called."

"But I don't think that would have changed Mrs. Marshall's mind," Stacey said. "She seemed definite about only wanting one sitter."

"But it's our rule that if it's over four kids, two of us go," Mary Anne pointed out. "They should know that."

"Should they?" Jessi asked. "I don't think I've ever told anyone that rule."

"Has anyone ever told a client the rule?" I asked.

No one replied.

"Maybe we should send a flier to our clients," Claudia suggested. "It could be really cute, and say something like, 'The Baby-sitters Club Golden Rules.' "

"That sounds good to me," I said. "And since you thought of it, Claud, and because you're our artist-in-residence, I say you should design it."

"Mine mith free." Claud's mouth was full of Malomars, but I was pretty certain that she said, "Fine with me."

Stacey crossed her arms and leaned back against Claud's headboard. "I still don't know what to do about the Marshalls. Since she said she only wanted one sitter, does that mean we should start refusing to baby-sit for her?"

"That's a tough one," I said, nibbling on the end of my pencil.

"We could just pretend that no one is available," Claudia suggested. "Then she won't think we don't want to sit for her."

Mary Anne cocked her head. "But that would be dishonest, wouldn't it?"

I would have liked to have discussed the

Marshall problem in more detail but the phone started ringing. By the time our half hour was up, Mallory was set to watch the Prezzioso girls Thursday afternoon and Stacey had agreed to take care of the Arnold twins Thursday evening. Mary Anne said she'd sit for the Hobart boys and Jessi agreed to watch Norman and Sara Hill.

As we adjourned the meeting, I told Stacey, "Don't worry too much about Mrs. Marshall. That's a problem the club will handle together."

"But how?" she asked.

"That's what we need to figure out."

CHAPTER 12

On the first of February, Karen marched through the front door and announced, "Daddy, we're here. You can get better now."

Watson was thrilled to see Karen and Andrew, and I actually think he did feel even better having them around. After one week, he really looked like the old Watson. He was laughing more, and even getting a bit more exercise, if you can count playing hide-and-seek in that huge house exercise. (I do. Running up and down those stairs can really wear you out!)

We had one week of perfect bliss. Then the Brewer-Thomas household came apart at the seams. I guess we should have seen it coming, what with Nannie moving out, and two more kids moving in, and the laundry piling up. But none of us did. One day, things just exploded.

The day began all wrong, with the entire household getting out of bed on the wrong side. Emily Michelle had the flu, and had spent half the night throwing up. Watson and Mom took turns staying up with her and by morning Watson was bleary-eyed. I overslept and wasn't able to help Mom and Watson get Andrew, Karen, and David Michael ready for school. Sam had forgotten to buy bread for sandwiches, so none of us could take a lunch to school. Then Andrew spilled his cereal during breakfast, and Karen had a complete meltdown.

Mom, who barely had time to get herself dressed, rushed into the kitchen like a general on a battlefield.

"Kristy, make sure the kids take their homework," she ordered. "Charlie, help the boys with their snow boots. Watson, don't forget to give Emily lots of water, and Sam, we're out of everything. Pick up some milk and bread at work this afternoon, would you?"

She didn't wait for anyone to respond but grabbed a cup of coffee and swept out the back door.

I couldn't find anyone's homework. Karen and Andrew had both lost the mates to their mittens and insisted we find them before

Karen went to school. Watson (the millionaire) didn't have enough change to give anybody their school lunch money. I had to break into my piggy bank. David Michael and Karen missed their buses. Then Charlie's car wouldn't start, so Watson piled everyone (including poor Emily Michelle) in the van and drove us to school. We were all late!

I tiptoed into homeroom and collapsed at my desk. Schoolwork — including a pop quiz in history — was easy compared to what had happened that morning. By the end of the school day, I had convinced myself that by the time I returned home, Mr. Mom would have everything under control again.

Boy, was I wrong!

I knew things were a problem before I even opened the front door. How? Andrew's coat and snow pants were lying outside on the front porch. When I pushed open the door, I was greeted by the sound of Emily Michelle crying upstairs, the television blaring in the den, and the phone ringing.

"Turn down that TV!" I shouted as I raced for the phone, tripping over the rest of Andrew's winter clothes.

"This is Mary at the office," a woman said when I answered. "May I speak with Mr. Brewer?"

"Just a minute," I said. "I'll see if I can find him."

I assumed Watson was with Emily so I called up the stairs, "Watson, are you there?"

He appeared on the landing, with Emily Michelle in his arms. A cloth diaper was draped over one shoulder and the apron he wore was splattered with what Emily must have had for lunch.

"Kristy, would you take Emily for a little while?" Watson asked in a exhausted voice. "She's having a tough time of it."

"Sure." I hurried up the stairs. Emily looked at me with tear-stained cheeks and said, "I want my bear."

"Come on, Em." I patted her gently on the back. "We'll go look in your room."

"Are Karen and Andrew downstairs?" Watson asked, as he untied the apron and dropped it in the bathroom sink.

"I think so," I replied. "The TV's on."

Watson hurried down the stairs. "I'd better check on them. They haven't had their afternoon snack."

I carried Emily toward her bedroom and suddenly remembered that Mary from the office was still waiting on the line. "Oh, my gosh! Watson!" I shouted. "There's a phone call for you."

126

"Tell them I have my hands full," Watson called from downstairs. "I'll get back to them as soon as I can."

I carried Emily Michelle to an upstairs extension, but when I picked up the phone, all I heard was a dial tone. "I guess Mary got tired of waiting," I whispered to Emily Michelle. "Oops."

Karen suddenly emerged from Mom's and Watson's bedroom, dressed in one of Mom's old party dresses and a pair of high heels. A big straw hat sat at a funny angle on her head.

"Hi, Kristy. Let's play Let's All Come In," she said, ready to swing right into the game. "I'll be Mrs. Fiddle-Faddle and you can be my maid."

"I'd love to, Karen, but I have to take care of Emily right now," I said. "Maybe Andrew can play."

"He hates Let's All Come In," Karen said, puffing out her lower lip. "Besides, we need four to play." Then she brightened and said, "Maybe Hannie can come over and play."

Hannie Papadakis lives across the street. Normally I would have thought that was a great idea, but this wasn't exactly a normal day.

"Not today, Karen. Emily's got the flu and we wouldn't want anyone else to catch it."

127

"Yeow!" Andrew howled from downstairs. "I hit my thumb."

"With what?" I asked, carrying Emily down the stairs.

Andrew stood in the living room, holding up a big hammer. "It really hurts," he cried.

"Andrew, where did you get that hammer?" I asked.

Watson raced into the room with a plate of cheese and crackers, a trail of Saltines spilling behind him. "That's my fault. I was going to do some laundry when I noticed the detergent shelf was loose. So I thought I'd fix it, but then Emily started to cry again, and I forgot about it."

Andrew ran crying to Watson, who said, "Come on, let's run that under some cold water in the kitchen."

Watson set the snack plate on the edge of the table, and didn't even notice that it tipped onto the floor as he left with Andrew.

Karen saw the food on the floor and wrinkled her nose. "My snack is all dirty. I can't eat that."

"I'll fix you another one," I said, scooping up the spilled crackers and shoving them back onto the plate.

"My bear," Emily moaned from my shoulder. "I want my bear."

128

"Karen, I'm going to need your help," I said, shifting Emily to my other shoulder. "We're having a little bit of a crisis here, so maybe you can help Watson with the snack. He'd like that."

Karen grinned. "I'll make some of my special Karen Brewer treats."

I watched her shuffle toward the kitchen in Mom's high heels. She tripped over a pile of laundry that had somehow made its way into the hall, but it didn't seem to faze her. She had a mission.

"I'm making Karen's special treats for everyone," she announced proudly before disappearing into the kitchen.

I took that opportunity to carry Emily Michelle back up the stairs. But just as we reached the top step, the front door swung open and Charlie stuck his head in the door.

"There are two packages from UPS sitting on the front porch," he called. "I think they're from Watson's office."

Watson called from the bathroom, "I've been expecting those. I wonder why they didn't ring the bell. Charlie, will you put them in the library?"

"Sure thing," Charlie replied. Moments later he shouted from inside the library, "Hey, Watson, your fax machine is going off and there's a stack of paper on the floor."

"Oh, gosh." Watson carried Andrew into the living room. "Will you be okay in here?"

Andrew, his eyes red from crying, nodded solemnly.

"Good boy." Watson patted him on the shoulder. "I have to make a few quick calls to my office, but I'll be right back."

Watson had vowed to leave the running of his office to his vice-presidents, but little by little he had been doing more and more work at home.

I heard the back door slam, and seconds later Sam came into the hall. "Hey, who left the phone off the hook?" he asked.

"I did," I said with a huge sigh. "There was a call for Watson, but things went a little nuts, and I forgot to tell him."

"I hope nobody was trying to call," he said, slipping the extension phone back on its hook.

I rolled my eyes. "They can just call back. And I'm sure they will. All we ever do around here is answer the phone."

"Boy, aren't we touchy?" Sam muttered.

I ignored his remark and asked, "Did you remember to pick up the bread?"

Sam hit his forehead and grimaced. "I forgot."

"Well, you better send Charlie for it," I

snapped. "Because I'm not going to raid my piggy bank again for school lunch money."

I headed back up the stairs with Emily Michelle, who was now fast asleep on my shoulder. I guess she'd given up on finding her teddy bear. After tucking her into her toddler bed, I hurried back to the kitchen to start dinner.

"Yikes!" I cried as I entered the kitchen. "What happened?"

Big globs of blueberry jam were all over the floor. Karen was on her knees, attempting to scoop them back into the jar with a baby spoon. "I had an accident," Karen answered. "But nothing broke."

"What were you doing?"

"I was going to make Karen's Special Jelly Roll-ups. But I couldn't find any bread. When I tried to look on the top shelf of the cupboard, I dropped the jelly." Karen shrugged. "I guess I will just have to make peanut butter graham cracker sandwiches."

I stepped over the jelly smears and reached for the refrigerator door. "Why don't we skip the snacks," I suggested, "and I'll start dinner early."

The refrigerator was almost empty except for a couple of jars of mustard, a few apples, and half-empty cartons of milk and juice. The vegetable drawer held a head of wilting lettuce. I checked the freezer.

"Frozen pizza," I murmured. "That's the best bet for tonight."

The phone rang. It was Mary from Watson's office again. She asked for Watson, adding, "Don't forget this time, okay?"

I set the frozen pizza on the counter, hopped over the jam, and ran to look for Watson. He was at his computer, typing up a memo.

"My bear!" I heard a little voice whimper behind me. Emily Michelle had gotten out of bed and scooted down the stairs to the library.

"Oh, Emily!" I scooped her up in my arms. Her forehead was hot. "Why don't we get you some juice, and then we'll go look for that bear."

"I'll get the juice," Charlie offered as we passed him in the hall.

And Karen, who was in the living room with Andrew, called out, "Has anybody seen David Michael?"

"David Michael!" Charlie and I shouted at the same moment.

"What time is it?" I checked my watch. "His play practice finished an hour ago. We forgot to pick him up."

"I'm on my way." Charlie raced out the door without stopping to put on his coat.

132

"This is terrible," I moaned. "Just terrible. Poor David Michael." Then I yelled, "Pick up the bread and milk while you're out, okay?"

Emily could tell I was worried and it upset her. "David Michael," she wailed.

Andrew heard her crying and he started whimpering, too. "My thumb hurts. It still hurts."

"I need some help here," Karen howled from the kitchen. "This jelly is not cooperating one bit."

I couldn't take it any more. I took a deep breath and shouted, "Watson? *Help!*"

"What in heaven's name is going on here?" Mom stood in the front door, a look of dismay on her face.

"Everything," I wailed. "Our house has completely come unglued."

Luckily for all of us, Mom took over. She found Emily's teddy bear, soothed Andrew, stuffed the laundry back in the hamper, cleaned up Karen's mess, and slipped the pizza into the oven. She even hung up the phone that was beeping in the front hall. (Poor Mary. I didn't think I'd ever be able to face her again.)

The pizza took thirty minutes to cook. Mom spent most of that time calming David Michael, who was really upset when Charlie brought him home. "I thought you forgot me forever," he said accusingly. "And that I was going to have to go to an orphanage and eat split pea soup morning, noon, and night."

"How could we ever forget you?" Mom murmured, rocking him in her arms. "Forget our star? You're going to be famous. People for years to come will talk about the boy who played the Brementown rooster."

That seemed to cheer him up. By the time the pizza was done he'd turned his terrible wait into an adventure. But frankly, I felt that I was at the end of my rope.

I wasn't the only one. When Watson came in for dinner, he collapsed into his chair, clutching a fax in one hand and a diaper in the other.

"We need to hire a housekeeper," he said grimly. *"Now."*

I missed Nannie. We all did. It was hard to believe that she wasn't still living with us and making everything run smoothly. Even Karen and Andrew would forget sometimes and call up the stairs, "Nannie, I'm home!" or, "Nannie, come look at my drawing."

Sunday was my day to visit her. We were going to have an afternoon tea with crumpets. I was looking forward to our time together, the first since she'd moved out.

Charlie dropped me outside Nannie's apartment building at one o'clock on the dot. Nannie and I greeted each other as if we hadn't seen each other for years.

"Come in, Kristy, come in," she said, ushering me into her tiny apartment. "I want you to sit down and tell me every single thing that's happened in your life since I saw you last."

"Everything?"

All I could think of was that disastrous day at home when Emily had the flu and we forgot to pick David Michael up from play practice.

"Start with the family and then move on to school or whatever," Nannie said as she carried her best silver tray into the living room. (She reserves that tray only for special, *special* occasions.) "But before you begin, I should point out today's features — fresh crumpets, chocolate-filled croissants, and lemon sugar cookies."

My mouth was already watering. "I better start with the chocolate."

"Ah, yes." Nannie chuckled as she handed me a croissant. "Life's short. Eat chocolate first."

"Those are Claudia's sentiments exactly," I said with a giggle.

"Did Claudia finish that mixed media collage she was working on?" Nannie said. "I know it was due this week."

I nodded. (My mouth was full of yummy chocolate and pastry.)

"And speaking of this week," Nannie continued, "isn't David Michael in dress rehearsals for *The Brementown Musicians*?"

"I don't know," I said, trying to remember if I'd seen it on our crowded family calendar.

136

"I'm not even sure when his play opens."

"Next Saturday," Nannie said firmly. "I plan to be there in the front row."

It was weird hearing her talk as if she would be going separately from our family. Suddenly I was hit by a huge wave of missing her.

"Oh, Nannie!" I put my croissant down. "I wish you were still with us. I mean, I know you need to be by yourself and you want your freedom and all that. But I miss you. We all miss you. Especially Emily. She wanders around the house, asking, 'Where Nannie?'"

Nannie's eyes filled with tears and she looked away from me. "I think I'll just get us a little more tea," she said, standing up and hurrying toward her kitchen.

I stared down at my full cup. I hadn't meant to make her feel bad, but I was just missing her so much. I decided I'd better change the subject. "You know, Karen and Andrew are at the big house now."

Nannie came back with the teapot. "Don't forget Karen's eye appointment. It's this Tuesday."

"You're amazing, Nannie," I said, shaking my head. "You're not even at the house and you've got it together. We live there and can't keep *anything* together."

"Oh?" Nannie sat down. "Aren't things going smoothly?"

"Smoothly?" I laughed out loud. "It's a disaster. Kids are running in and out. Coats and boots are everywhere. The phone rings all the time for Watson, and his office is sending more faxes than he can deal with. He tries to keep up with the laundry — we all do — but with two more kids, it's practically impossible."

"I thought Watson had cut back on his work," Nannie said, frowning.

"He tried to. But it's hard for him. His office really needs his help."

"Who's taking care of the kids?"

"Watson watches Emily Michelle and Andrew, when he's not in preschool," I explained, "and we've all taken turns picking up David Michael from play practice. But now that Karen and Andrew are here it's pretty wild."

"Is there anything I can do to help?" Nannie asked, taking a sip of her tea but keeping her eyes on me.

"Well . . ."

What I wanted to do was yell, "Yes! Come back, please!" Instead I stammered, "Um, maybe you — you could help us find a, uh, a housekeeper."

"Housekeeper!" Nannie set her cup down

on her saucer so hard that tea sloshed over the sides, but she didn't seem to notice. "You don't need a housekeeper."

"But we do," I protested. "I mean, we're all trying to help out the best we can, but with Mom at work and Watson trying to work, well, things are really falling apart. We forget to buy groceries. We've had to order out for pizza two nights in a row."

"What?" Nannie stood up and began pacing the room. "This will never do. I mean, it's just not right. Emily Michelle needs someone to give her her full attention. You all do."

"That's right," I said. "But who?"

Nannie put her hands on her hips. "How about me?"

"Oh, Nannie!" I leapt to my feet and threw my arms around her. "Would you really come back?"

"Of course," Nannie replied with a smile. "That is, if you're sure you need me."

"We've *always* needed you," I cried. "I thought you wanted to be by yourself."

"Oh, fiddle," she said, waving her hand. "Who wants to be alone? Certainly not this old lady. I love being with you kids."

I was confused. "But why did you leave us?"

"I thought you didn't need me anymore,"

139

Nannie confessed. "Since Watson had decided to stay home, I was afraid I would be in the way. You know, step on his toes."

"That's ridiculous!" I put my hands on my hips. "And you know it. Watson can do a lot of things but he can't keep everyone's schedules in his head, and he can never remember who likes what for breakfast. And you should see what he packs in the kids' lunches — sardine sandwiches."

"Sardines! Oh, my word." Nannie was thoroughly tickled. "I bet that smelled to high heaven."

"Karen was humiliated at school," I said with a chuckle, "and swore she'd never take one of his bag lunches again."

"Oh, my!" Nannie laughed and nodded her head. "It does sound like you need me. It most certainly does."

I took Nannie's hand eagerly. "Come on. Let's go talk to Mom and Watson right now. They're home."

"But what will they think?" Nannie said, hesitating. "One minute I move out, and the next minute I move back in."

"What will they think?" I repeated. "They'll be thrilled, ecstatic, grateful, delirious with happiness. Nannie, we all miss you terribly."

Nannie put one hand to her mouth, trying

to keep her lip from trembling. "And I miss you, too. These Waterford Gardens are driving me batty. I need some action. I need some noise!"

I carried the tray of goodies into her kitchen and set them on the counter. Then I grabbed our coats from the closet. "Let's go talk to Mom and Watson now."

And that's what we did. Nannie and I hopped in the Pink Clinker and off we went.

The second Nannie walked in the front door, the kids appeared from everywhere. It was as if she were a magnet. David Michael wrapped his arms around her legs and wouldn't let go. Emily Michelle just kept patting Nannie's face and shoulders, as if to make sure it really was her. Karen and Andrew, Charlie and Sam and I — we clustered around her, happy to have her there.

Watson and Mom were reading the Sunday papers in the den. When they heard the commotion, they came to the door to see what was going on. Nannie beamed at them from the center of her kid huddle. "Hi, you two. I'd like to talk to you about a mistake I think I may have made."

Mom's eyes widened and she looked at me. I nodded happily. "Nannie wants to come back."

"Oh, Mother!" Mom joined the circle of hugging kids. "Why did you ever leave?"

"Well. I guess I had a moment of silliness and thought I might not be wanted anymore," Nannie said.

"That must have been my fault," Watson said with a rueful grin. "But, Nannie, we not only want you — we need you. Please, won't you come home?"

Karen, Andrew, and David Michael raised their faces to look at Nannie.

"Please?" David Michael pleaded.

"You've got to," Karen added.

This time Nannie couldn't stop her tears. "Of course I will," she murmured, dabbing at her eyes.

After a lot of hugging and kissing and apologizing, it was decided that Nannie would come home as soon as possible. Moving day was set for Wednesday. Only three days away!

CHAPTER 14

"This meeting of the BSC is officially called to order," I announced on Monday.

A big smile must have been plastered all over my face because Claudia said, "Kristy's either in love or she won the lottery."

"Sort of both," I said. "Nannie, whom I love, is moving back in with us and, boy, that feels like we've won the big prize."

Mary Anne looked at me with watery eyes (I told you, she cries at cat food commercials). "Kristy, I'm so happy for you. I know you missed Nannie a lot."

"It's funny. Nannie's move would never have happened if everyone had said what was on their minds right at the beginning," I said. "I mean, Nannie actually thought we didn't need her."

"That's silly," Stacey commented. "It's so obvious that she *is* needed. And wanted."

"Obvious to everyone but Nannie," I replied. "Plus, Watson and Mom were afraid to tell Nannie that, because they didn't want to interfere with her plans. When she told them she wanted a place of her own, they believed her."

"You know," Dawn said, cocking her head, "maybe that's our problem with Mrs. Marshall. We just assumed she knew about our two-sitter rule."

Claud nodded. "When we sent two of us over without telling her, she was really miffed."

"I think we should definitely send out those fliers Claud suggested," Mary Anne said. "But we should also make it a club policy to ask how many children we'll be baby-sitting for whenever a client calls."

"That way people will know that they can't just add a few kids without telling us," Mallory finished.

"That still leaves us with the Mrs. Marshall problem," Jessi pointed out. "I mean, we can send her a flier, but shouldn't one of us talk to her?"

The club agreed that we should. Then everyone turned to face me.

"I think you should make the call," Claudia said. "Because you're the club president."

I looked carefully at each face. My friends were watching to see what I was going to do. I knew I had to make that call. Especially after the speech I'd just made about the importance of speaking up now rather than later.

"Okay." I reached for the phone. "I'll do it."

Mary Anne read me the number and I dialed. Two rings later Mrs. Marshall picked up the phone. My heart instantly started pounding in my chest.

"Um, Mrs. Marshall? This is Kristy Thomas."

"Yes, Kristy. What is it?"

Mrs. Marshall sounded awfully stiff.

"I want to apologize for sending two sitters to the job last week."

"Yes, that was a bit of a surprise. Especially when Stacey walked out on me when I said I wouldn't pay for both of them."

Mrs. Marshall wasn't making this easy.

"Yes, well, we had all assumed that you knew about our policy of always using two sitters for more than four kids."

"I didn't know about it," Mrs. Marshall replied. "But I guess I do now."

"We're mailing fliers to our clients to make sure there aren't any more misunderstandings," I explained. "Also, we're making it a

145

policy to ask how many children we'll be expected to care for when a client calls."

"Yes, I guess that is good for the sitter to know." Mrs. Marshall was finally starting to warm up and sound like her old self.

"We like to be prepared," I continued. "When we know who we're going to sit for, we can plan activities, and stock our Kid-Kits with the appropriate supplies."

There was a pause on the other end of the line.

"I think I owe you an apology, too," Mrs. Marshall said. "For springing the Phillips children on you. I honestly didn't think it would be a problem. And I forgot how professional you really are."

I gave my friends the thumbs-up sign. "Thanks, Mrs. Marshall. We do our best."

"I hope your club will still sit for Nina and Eleanor. They're very fond of you."

"Sure we will," I replied. "We really like them, too."

"In that case," Mrs. Marshall continued, "as long as I have you on the phone — could I reserve a sitter for tomorrow afternoon?"

"For your jazzercize class?" I asked.

"Oh, no," Mrs. Marshall answered with a laugh. "I've discovered that jazzercize isn't my thing. I've decided to try water aerobics. And don't worry, Mrs. Phillips' kids won't be here. She hates to swim."

"So that's two kids, Tuesday afternoon."

"From four to five-thirty," Mrs. Marshall said.

"We'll check the schedule and call you right back."

I hung up the phone and grinned at my friends. "Problem solved. Mrs. Marshall even apologized for having the Phillips kids at her house without telling us."

"Phew!" Stacey and Claudia fell against each other in relief.

"I was afraid she'd hate me forever," Stacey giggled.

"She doesn't hate any of us," I said. "In fact she wants one of us to sit for her tomorrow. Mary Anne? What does the magic book tell us?"

Mary Anne smiled as she ran her finger down her schedule. "The magic book tells me that this is a job for you, Kristy. You're the only one who doesn't have a conflict."

"Great!"

The next day I arrived at the Marshalls' fully prepared. I'd stocked my Kid-Kit with paper dolls for Nina, and a couple of David Michael's old wooden puzzles for Eleanor.

"Kristy, it's good to see you," Mrs. Marshall

said warmly when she opened the door. "I've left the number at the pool by the phone and the kids have asked if you would make them grilled cheese sandwiches for dinner."

"I think I can manage that," I said.

Mrs. Marshall leaned in and whispered, "They asked for that because the last time you made them, you used cookie cutters to cut the sandwiches into stars and moons."

"We can do that again," I whispered back. "And maybe make some fun faces on top."

Mrs. Marshall smiled. "Well, I know they're in good hands."

Hearing her say that really made my day. The rest of the afternoon was a breeze. We played with the paper dolls for a long time, and while Eleanor didn't actually put the puzzle pieces back in the puzzle, she sure enjoyed tossing them around.

At dinnertime, I pulled out all the stops.

"Ladies and tots, take your seats and prepare to be amazed."

The girls eagerly scooted into their chairs at the kitchen table.

"I will attempt to flip not one, but *two* cheese sandwiches in the air with only one flipper."

Actually I'd never tried it before but I figured if the sandwich landed crooked it would still be fun. To my surprise, and Nina and Eleanor's delight, I actually managed to flip both grilled cheese sandwiches in the air and catch them in the frying pan.

Then, instead of using cookie cutters, I grabbed a couple of water glasses and let the girls use the upside-down glasses to make their own "cheesy suns" out of their sandwiches.

"Here are some raisins," I said, checking in the cupboard. "We can put faces on our suns. You can attach them with a small glop of peanut butter."

"Peanut butter, cheese, and raisins?" Nina repeated, wrinkling her nose.

Eleanor saw her sister's face and blurted out, "Yuck!"

That made everyone giggle. We spent the rest of the meal inventing the worst food combinations we could imagine. The winners were pickles, onions, and honey, and, rhino toes and snake-eye sandwiches. *Major* yuck!

CHAPTER 15

"Nannie's here!" Karen ran through the house making her announcement on Wednesday afternoon. "Everybody, Nannie's here!"

Once again, the family gathered on the front porch. It was strange to have two homecomings in such a short period. First Watson, and now Nannie. But Nannie's arrival was quite a bit different.

The moment the Pink Clinker rounded the corner onto McLelland Street, Nannie hit the car horn. She didn't stop honking until she pulled into the drive.

"Look out, world!" Nannie shouted out the window. "Nannie's back!"

We watched as she flung open the door and leapt in the air. "Ta-da!"

"Hooray for Nannie!" I led the cheering as Emily Michelle and the rest of the kids raced down the porch steps to hug her.

"She's just what the doctor ordered!" Watson chuckled.

Charlie and Sam were following Nannie in the U-Haul truck. They'd heard Nannie's honk and decided to do the same. The truck beep-beeped its way up the street, bringing several neighbors onto their front lawns to see what all the commotion was about.

It was most definitely a day for celebrating. The unloading of the truck was totally silly. Sam would announce, "Nannie's rocker!" and then Charlie would cry, "Let's hear it for Nannie's rocker. Hip, hip, hooray!"

"Nannie's cedar trunk! Hooray for the trunk!"

The kids loved it. They cheered as loudly as any pep club at a football game. And it was all for Nannie. Boy, were we glad to have her home.

That evening at dinner, Watson officially welcomed Nannie back with a special toast. Then he made another announcement.

"I'm especially glad that Nannie has returned," he began, "because it allows me to make a choice that I feel needs to be made."

I looked over at Mom and saw a confused look on her face. Whatever Watson was up to was news to her, too.

"As you all know, since I've been home, the

calls and faxes from Unity have increased. It's become pretty clear to me that I can't just quit working, so I've made a decision — "

"Oh, Watson," Mom cut in, "you're not going back to work, are you? Your health! Long hours, no more weekends — "

Watson held up his hand. "Before you give yourself a heart attack, Elizabeth," he said with a mischievous grin, "let me finish."

Mom smiled sheepishly. "Sorry."

"What I've come up with is a happy compromise. I'm going to work part-time here at home. I'll set up a complete home office, and three hours a day, I'll handle what needs to be done at Unity. But the other twenty-one hours will be devoted totally to my family."

"Me!" Emily Michelle cried.

"That's right, sweetie." Watson ruffled Emily's hair. "I really like being Mr. Mom and now that Nannie, the super grandmother, has come home for good, I think we can put some sanity back into our lives."

"Sanity?" Nannie joked. "I hope you're not expecting *that*."

Just to be silly, she balanced her spoon on the tip of her nose. Of course, that meant we all had to try it. Within seconds spoons were clattering onto the table and floor. Mom kept trying to restore order but she was laughing too hard to be taken seriously.

That set the tone for the entire evening. After dinner, we played team Monopoly. (No, Watson wasn't the banker. I was.) And then we gathered in Nannie's room to say good night.

Life really did return to normal at our house. Watson set up his office and kept his promise to work only three hours a day. He and Nannie worked out a perfect system, taking turns cooking and chauffeuring kids, until they had the house running like clockwork.

Meanwhile, Nannie put the final touches on David Michael's rooster costume, and we all readied ourselves for his big opening night.

Ever since Charlie and I had forgotten to pick David Michael up at rehearsal, we'd made a special effort to be extra sensitive to his feelings. We decided to make this opening night a Brewer/Thomas extravaganza.

I handed out the assignments (naturally) and Charlie did the driving. Karen and Andrew made "Good Cluck On Your Opening" cards, complete with glitter glue. I picked out flowers for a bouquet, and Sam filled a plastic rooster that he'd gotten at the Goodwill store with M&M's. Mom made sure she had plenty of film for the camera, and Watson practiced his shooting techniques with the camcorder.

On opening night, our family took up the entire front row! When David Michael made his first entrance onto the stage, Emily Michelle cried out in her high-pitched voice, Arr-er-arr-er-*rooo*!'' The audience burst out laughing.

It threw David Michael for just a second but he soon got back on track. When he said his now famous line, ''Cock-a-doodle-doo! I'm a musician, too!'' I actually cried. (I know that sounds like something Mary Anne would do. I couldn't help myself.) I could hear sniffles all the way down the row. Watson, who was recording it all on camera, had to dab at his eyes. Mom and Nannie just held hands and wept happy tears.

We cried because the play was so cute. But we also cried because our family had been through a lot together over the past few weeks. It had been a really rough stretch but we'd made it. Watson, our own Mr. Mom, was now healthy and very happy, Nannie was home for good, and David Michael, my wonderful little brother, was the star of the show.

About the Author

ANN M. MARTIN did *a lot* of baby-sitting when she was growing up in Princeton, New Jersey. She is a former editor of books for children, and was graduated from Smith College.

Ms. Martin lives in New York City with her cats, Mouse and Rosie. She likes ice cream and *I Love Lucy*; and she hates to cook.

Ann Martin's Apple Paperbacks include *Yours Turly, Shirley*; *Ten Kids, No Pets*; *With You and Without You*; *Bummer Summer*; and all the other books in the Baby-sitters Club series.

Look for #82

JESSI AND THE TROUBLEMAKER

Danielle, Greg, and Mary Anne went through the contents of the Kid-Kit until Charlotte and Haley arrived. Then Mary Anne and Greg settled down with a book that instantly caught Greg's attention, *Freckle Juice*, while Charlotte, Haley, and Danielle disappeared into Danielle's room.

I was quiet for awhile. In spite of the short notice and the rush to get to the Robertses', Mary Anne began to feel mellow.

Until it happened.

Not a disaster on the Jackie Rodowsky scale. Not an accident, either. It was a pretty interesting idea — if you weren't the baby-sitter.

It started with an odd whump-thumping. At first Mary Anne thought it was the pipes or just the random winter sounds a house makes. It wasn't enough to make her instincts go on alert.

When she heard it again, she wondered if a storm door was banging or a shutter was loose on the house. She decided to check it out.

"Excuse me for just a minute," she said to Greg.

The thumping was louder in the hall. And it was accompanied by muffled voices.

Mary Anne followed the sounds to the basement door. She heard a shriek, a giggle, and more thumping. She pulled the door open and found herself in —

Aspen, Colorado.

Not really. But Danielle, Charlotte, and Haley *had* brought a little of the great outdoors inside.

They were sledding down the basement stairs. Using what looked like the mattress from a crib.

As Mary Anne opened the door, Charlotte took off thumping and bumping down the stairs. She landed at the bottom with a muffled shriek and Danielle's voice said, "Awesome, Char. You went almost all the way to the furnace."

"My turn," Haley's voice said. "Help me carry the sled back up the sta . . ." Her voice trailed off. She had spotted Mary Anne.

**Read all the books
about Kristy
in the Baby-sitters Club series
by Ann M. Martin**

THE BABY-SITTERS CLUB®

by Ann M. Martin

More titles... ▶

The Baby-sitters Club titles continued...

❑ MG45659-8	#58 Stacey's Choice	$3.50
❑ MG45660-1	#59 Mallory Hates Boys (and Gym)	$3.50
❑ MG45662-8	#60 Mary Anne's Makeover	$3.50
❑ MG45663-6	#61 Jessi's and the Awful Secret	$3.50
❑ MG45664-4	#62 Kristy and the Worst Kid Ever	$3.50
❑ MG45665-2	#63 Claudia's ~~Freind~~ Friend	$3.50
❑ MG45666-0	#64 Dawn's Family Feud	$3.50
❑ MG45667-9	#65 Stacey's Big Crush	$3.50
❑ MG47004-3	#66 Maid Mary Anne	$3.50
❑ MG47005-1	#67 Dawn's Big Move	$3.50
❑ MG47006-X	#68 Jessi and the Bad Baby-Sitter	$3.50
❑ MG47007-8	#69 Get Well Soon, Mallory!	$3.50
❑ MG47008-6	#70 Stacey and the Cheerleaders	$3.50
❑ MG47009-4	#71 Claudia and the Perfect Boy	$3.50
❑ MG47010-8	#72 Dawn and the We Love Kids Club	$3.50
❑ MG45575-3	Logan's Story Special Edition Readers' Request	$3.25
❑ MG47118-X	Logan Bruno, Boy Baby-sitter Special Edition Readers' Request	$3.50
❑ MG44240-6	Baby-sitters on Board! Super Special #1	$3.95
❑ MG44239-2	Baby-sitters' Summer Vacation Super Special #2	$3.95
❑ MG43973-1	Baby-sitters' Winter Vacation Super Special #3	$3.95
❑ MG42493-9	Baby-sitters' Island Adventure Super Special #4	$3.95
❑ MG43575-2	California Girls! Super Special #5	$3.95
❑ MG43576-0	New York, New York! Super Special #6	$3.95
❑ MG44963-X	Snowbound Super Special #7	$3.95
❑ MG44962-X	Baby-sitters at Shadow Lake Super Special #8	$3.95
❑ MG45661-X	Starring the Baby-sitters Club Super Special #9	$3.95
❑ MG45674-1	Sea City, Here We Come! Super Special #10	$3.95

Available wherever you buy books...or use this order form.

Scholastic Inc., P.O. Box 7502, 2931 E. McCarty Street, Jefferson City, MO 65102

Please send me the books I have checked above. I am enclosing $_____
(please add $2.00 to cover shipping and handling). Send check or money order - no cash or C.O.D.s please.

Name _____ Birthdate_____

Address _____

City_____ State/Zip _____
Please allow four to six weeks for delivery. Offer good in the U.S. only. Sorry, mail orders are not available to residents of Canada. Prices subject to change.

BSC993

Ann Martin wants *YOU* to help name the new baby-sitter...and her twin.

*Dear Diary,
I'm 13 now...finally in the 8th grade. My twin sister and I just moved here and this great group of girls asked me to join their baby-sitting club...*

Name the twins and win a

THE BABY SITTERS CLUB

book dedication!

Simply dream up the first and last names of the new baby-sitter and her twin sister (who's not in the BSC), and fill in the names on the coupon below. One lucky entry will be selected by Ann M. Martin and Scholastic Inc. The winning names will continue to be featured in the series starting next fall 1995, and the winner will have a future BSC book dedicated to her/him!

THE BSC NAME THE TWINS CONTEST

Name the new twins! (First and last, please)

_____ **and** _____

Name _____ Birthdate _____
                                              M / D / Y

Street _____ City _____ State/Zip _____

BSCC1194

Create Your Own Mystery Stories!

THE BABY-SITTERS CLUB®

MYSTERY GAME !

WHO: Boyfriend **WHY:** Romance
WHAT: Phone Call **WHERE:** Dance

Use the special Mystery Case card to pick WHO did it, WHAT was involved, WHY it happened and WHERE it happened. Then dial secret words on your Mystery Wheels to add to the story! Travel around the special Stoneybrook map gameboard to uncover your friends' secret word clues! Finish four baby-sitting jobs and find out all the words to win. Then have everyone join in to tell the story!